HebrewPunk

ALSO BY LAVIE TIDHAR

NOVELS
*The Tel Aviv Dossier**
*Osama**
The Violent Century
*A Man Lies Dreaming**
Unholy Land
By Force Alone
The Candy Mafia

THE BOOKMAN HISTORIES
The Bookman
Camera Obscura
The Great Game
(also available in omnibus form as *The Bookman Histories*)

NOVELLAS
*An Occupation of Angels**
*New Atlantis**
*The Vanishing Kind**
*Cloud Permutations**
*Jesus & the Eightfold Path**
*Gorel & the Pot-Bellied God**

COLLECTIONS
*Black Gods Kiss**
*HebrewPunk**
The Apex Book of World SF (as editor)
The Apex Book of World SF 2 (as editor)
The Apex Book of World SF 3 (as editor)

*available as a JABberwocky ebook

HEBREWPUNK

Lavie Tidhar

JABberwocky Literary Agency, Inc.

HebrewPunk
Copyright © 2007, 2016 by Lavie Tidhar
Originally published in 2007 by Apex Publications
This paperback edition published in 2023 by JABberwocky Literary Agency, Inc.
"The Heist" first published in *The Horror Express*, 2005
"Transylvanian Mission" first published in *Dark Lurkers*, 2004
"The Dope Fiend" first published in *Sci Fiction*, 2005
"Uganda" first published in *HebrewPunk* (Apex edition), 2007
"The Women of 1926" by James Laver © James Laver,
published by arrangement with David Higham Associates
Cover art and design © 2023 by Paul McCaffrey
All rights reserved.

ISBN 978-1-625676-25-2

Published by JABberwocky Literary Agency, Inc.
49 W. 45th Street, Suite #5N
New York, NY 10036
awfulagent.com/ebooks

AUTHOR'S
INTRODUCTION

I wrote *HebrewPunk* over a fairly long period of time, with the first story, "The Heist" probably dating as far back as 2003 or so, and the last, "Uganda," written especially for the collection around 2006 or 2007. It began, rather simply, as a sort of tongue-in-cheek parody of pulp fiction tropes in "The Heist," based around the premise that Jewish vampires would be immune to the traditional threats facing fictional ones—crosses and holy water being the most obvious. As soon as I wrote that first story, I had a light bulb moment, realising that each of the three characters introduced therein—the rabbi, the rat and the tzaddik—deserved their own stories, and that these stories, more seriously, should engage in some form with questioning the underlying assumptions of the traditional pulp milieus they were to operate in. I set down some other ground rules. Each story would be set in a different period of 20th century Jewish history. And each would consciously emulate a different form of pulp fiction—a WW2 adventure in "Transylvanian

Mission"; a "dope fiend" story in "The Dope Fiend"; a lost world story in "Uganda" ("The Heist," of course, is a heist caper). In a way, I realise now, the stories serve as an early model for the work I would later take on in novels such as *The Violent Century* (which borrows liberally for one section from "Transylvanian Mission") and *A Man Lies Dreaming*. The historical element of those three stories was important to me. My own visit to Transylvania many years ago, where my family originates from, inspired the work on that story. For "The Dope Fiend," I had first-hand knowledge of many of the locales, and as with the other stories, all the history is real. For "Uganda," I had to travel to a private library in London where I could view the original report of the Zionist expedition to East Africa on microfilm, and the writing was inspired by my own travels in East and Central Africa. I would revisit it later, in more depth, in my novel *Unholy Land*.

Although originally published individually, I intended from the start for the stories to stand as a unified collection, and was fortunate that Jason Sizemore of Apex was supportive of my idea (as, indeed, he has been of many of my ridiculous plans). Since *HebrewPunk*'s original 2007 publication, the stories have also appeared in Hebrew, Polish, and Hungarian magazines, been adapted to audio, and the term 'HebrewPunk' (itself, naturally, very much tongue-in-cheek) made its way, improbably enough, into the Encyclopedia Judaica. In many ways, *HebrewPunk* stands as an early model for work I will continue to develop in different forms for years afterwards. I am delighted to issue this new edition of the collection, with new cover art by Paul McCaffrey, in the hope it remains available to any reader interested in such tales. I hope you enjoy the book!

THE HEIST

The most consciously pulp driven story in this collection, and the earliest, it first introduces the main characters in a sort of parody of both dark fantasy and heist capers. It was this story that acted—as often happens to me—as the "seed" for the collection, from which the other stories sprang.

BREACH

The bank stands alone at the city's heart. Circular and tall, its face to the world is of unbroken, smooth steel, a façade that hides and protects its heart. Whatever windows there may be are hidden.

Along its vertical wall a shadow moves. Where no living creature could go it crawls, a piece of darkness and moonlight almost indistinguishable from its surroundings.

It moves along. Its body is encased in a darkness that is more than clothes; its hands cling to the wall by uncertain means. It climbs the tower like a spider, scuttling in a silence that is more than the absence of noise.

The tower's immune system has not so far detected the intruder. If it had, hidden machines would open fire, for every five lead bullets two of silver, for every four bullets one tipped with gold. If it had, if the motion sensors and the heat sensors, the dust sensors and the X-ray sensors, radar and cameras and other, more arcane means, have not temporarily failed, the intruder would be captured and brought inside to the intimate womb of the tower, from which it would never return.

The intruder moves, uninterrupted, until it reaches the upper levels of the tower. Here there are hidden windows, a loose array of armoured, one way mirrors.

The intruder feels along the sides of one, running its hands along the perimeter of the small window. Any impact with the glass, any cut made to the layers of glass and wiring, will cause an immediate reaction. It jerks away its hand in seeming pain: there are tiny crucifixes cut into the glass, every five centimetres. The intruder scuttles up and down the side of the wall until it finds a window that it is apparently satisfied with. Feeling along the bottom of the windows, it detects the tiniest motion of air. There is a gap in the tower, a breach on a micronic scale.

In seconds, the intruder is gone. A cloud of vapour hangs in the air for a short while yet, the ghost of the dark mist that edges its way into the tower.

Inside, the cloud quickly reassembles. It reveals its shape first, then solidifies further, now that it is in the building. The intruder's clothes are matte black, sealing the body inside it.

The intruder removes its headgear, revealing the face of a woman. She glides along the walls and down a corridor, looking around her cautiously. Her movements are precise.

There are no sounds. Her steps become more confident as she walks further into the heart of the tower.

Then, without warning, dark shapes slide out of the ceiling.

They look like bulbous plants at first, little metal balls that noiselessly grow a circle of tiny pipes around themselves, like the offshoots of a flower.

They sprinkle out water in a fine mist that gently descends to the floor. The intruder does not even notice until the water is nearly on her naked face.

Then she screams.

In the dim light of the corridor her face is a mask of writhing shadows. Where the water touches it, the skin blisters and frays.

Only the eyes remain for a while longer as the face around them is rapidly consumed, staring with an unnatural fear at the floating mist. Then they, too, are consumed in a bright flare and her whole head explodes, spraying the walls with brain and blood that are dry, and that form little mounds of mud on the floor. The intruder's body slowly topples over.

In time it, too, is consumed by the mist.

INTERLUDE

Somewhere, a phone rings. A large, hairy hand picks up the receiver. A Chopin concerto is playing loudly in the background.

"Yes?" The speaker is sitting in an armchair, looking out of a large window on the city that sprawls underneath. It is early morning, and the sun is already burning.

"We failed."

"So I gather." There's a newspaper spread on the man's knees.

"Last night," he says, his dry voice echoing down the line, "a burglar attempted to gain entry to the blood bank's premises. The intruder was apprehended by bank security and killed while violently trying to resist arrest." He pauses. "But we know what really happened, don't we?"

The voice on the other side of the phone sounds tired. "They tell you at the bottom of the article," he says. "I think. A friendly little warning from the authorities."

The man's finger traces the lines of text. "Incidentally, we have recently learned that the automated fire-prevention system recently installed at the blood bank carries water blessed by a high-ranking member of the clergy." He can see the tall tower of the bank from his window, shining coolly in the bright sunlight.

"Holy water sprinklers?" His voice is even, but cannot totally disguise that the man is impressed.

"Another one bites the dust."

"Quite." The man sits quietly for a few moments as musical notes chase each other around the room. "Find me someone who can do it," he says. "Anyone."

He puts the phone down, gently.

CORPORATE POLITICS

"Yes, sir," Jiminy says, even though the line is dead. Jiminy is balding, with unruly tufts of hair sticking out of his head like wildfire. His face is grey and lined. There are dark patches of sweat on his suit, under his armpits.

From his office window he can see the abandoned docks and the river. The dark water foams, churning out a familiar, almost welcome stench.

"The boss ain't happy," he says to the short man leaning against the wall. His tone is accusing. The man shrugs, a gesture of carelessness that infuriates Jiminy.

He grabs the short man and kicks him in the groin. The man falls to the ground. Jiminy's hands shake. "Listen, you little *shit*," he whispers. "If the boss ain't happy then I ain't happy." He kicks the man in the ribs, hard. "And if I ain't happy then you *certainly* ain't happy." He grabs the man's hair and forces his head up, sharply. "Especially seeing as it was *your* burglar that just got vaporised." He slaps the man hard with the back of his hand.

"I want results this time, sunshine," he whispers. "Or it's your time to start looking for some prime real estate at the bottom of the river, 'cause that's where you will be relocating to on a permanent basis real soon. Understand?"

He drops the short man to the floor and kicks him one last time. "Now get out and fix it."

THE FIXER

"I know a man," the short man says. "A *macher*." His voice on the phone is hoarse.

Jiminy is chewing on a short cigar. He is still at his office. "A *macher*?"

"A fixer." The short man takes a deep breath. "Name of Cahana. Ezra Cahana. Known as The Rabbi."

"A Jew," Jiminy says. His hand is drumming a rapid beat on the oak desk.

The short man hesitates. "We've exhausted all other avenues," he says.

In the dark room Jiminy nods.

He thinks briefly, then speaks into the phone. "Where do I find him?"

It turns out the Rabbi doesn't travel. You want him, you come to him. Jiminy curses as he drives through the narrow streets of downtown, searching for the address. He pulls over outside a small house. The street lamps are unlit and the windows of the house are dim. Rats hurry through a mound of rubbish outside. In the light of the moon their fur looks blood-encrusted and dirty.

He pats his coat, reassuring himself of the gun's presence. He knocks on the door.

THE CAST

The Rabbi knows a few people. He opens a thick folder of brown paper and leafs through it. There's Yanek 'the Gondolier' Kozlovsky, a contract killer with a speciality in vampires who likes drowning his victims in vats of holy water. There's Motti the Shark, a rogue Kabbalist with a line in curses. There's Jimmy the Prophet, whose powers of divination allow him to burgle empty houses with an unnatural ease.

He knows a few people. He pulls three sheets from the folder and lays them on the table in front of Jiminy.

"Jimmy the Rat." His finger taps a staccato on the page. "Age unknown, though at least a hundred. A vampire, and, almost uniquely, a Jew." The Rabbi sighs, but it is not clear whether it is the idea of a Jewish vampire or its uniqueness that saddens him more. He continues. "Shape-shifting abilities—the moniker is not for nought—immunity from crosses, holy water and silver, although he is fatally affected by gold. A loner, naturally. Served with the partisans in Eastern Europe during the Holocaust, an expert with explosives, several posthumous medals for bravery."

He shifts his finger to the second sheet. "Frankie Bloomenthal, AKA The Tzaddik. Frankie is a Wandering Jew, and the rumour is he was once one of the *Lamed Vav*—the Thirty-Six Tzaddiks who preserve the order of the world. An unfortunate taste for expensive drugs and loose women. Immortal—naturally—he can be hurt but not stopped."

The Rabbi's finger shifts to the third sheet. "Lastly, one of my close associates. Strong—much more so than a human—obedient, extremely loyal and very quiet on his feet." He stares at a point directly behind Jiminy and smiles. "*Very* quiet."

When Jiminy turns round he has to control his hand, prevent it from reaching for the gun. There is a huge *thing* blocking the door, a man-shaped figure made of a dark, fluid material. It exudes menace like a pungent cologne.

"Goldie." The Rabbi says proudly.

"What is that thing?" Jiminy says. He takes a step back.

"A golem." The Rabbi Says. His smile is unpleasant. "Certain Rabbis, you see, can mould a human figure from clay and animate it."

His tone of voice makes it clear to which category of Rabbi he belongs. "It's done by writing down the true name of God and putting the paper under the golem's tongue."

Jiminy isn't going to argue with that, not with the golem standing right beside him.

The Rabbi continues. "Goldie is an improvement in several ways on a traditional golem, however," he says, "most importantly in his physical attributes. Instead of the traditional clay I've used a special mixture of clay, industrial diamonds and steel that can absorb double the impact of a standard golem, and produce three times the punch. In addition, the usually flat mouth has been enhanced with a special set of teeth. Smile, Goldie."

The giant golem opens its mouth. Sharp, artificial dentures shine in the dim light.

"Alternating gold, silver, and titanium alloy," the Rabbi says. "Can take on *anyone*. In addition," he continues, "certain modifications to the writing that animates Goldie have been made that provide him with a modicum of free will." The Rabbi shrugs. "A necessary requirement if one was to assist successfully in an unpredictable operation. Such as," he says evenly, "the operation you have in mind."

Jiminy has heard enough. "You'd better not fail," he says. Money changes hands.

Jiminy has to push past the golem on his way out. He takes a deep breath in the steamy air outside and hurries to his car.

RECRUITMENT

The Rabbi finds the Tzaddik at his favourite place, a nearly-empty bar whose dark interior is illuminated only by the dim light of the neon signs outside. The Tzaddik is sitting in the corner, a glass and bottle of wine on the table beside him.

The Rabbi sits down and places a second glass on the table. He murmurs a short prayer over the wine then pours himself a generous helping.

"Got a job for you," he says. The Tzaddik doesn't seem to hear him.

"The big job, Frankie—" the Rabbi's voice is excited "—this is it. The retirement fund, the bailout money, the big payout. Even for you."

The Tzaddik grips his wine glass. His fingers are long and pale, and hairless. Pigmentation spots are strewn across them haphazardly. He smiles crookedly at the Rabbi. "There is always one last job, Rabbi. Always one more." He empties his glass and stands up.

"And there will always be a Tzaddik to do them," the

Rabbi says. He tops up his glass. "Meet me at the warehouse tomorrow. Eight o'clock. Don't be late."

He drinks wine and watches the retreating back of the Tzaddik.

* * *

Jimmy the Rat hangs out at the Glass Tit, as bright as the Tzaddik's bar is dark. The night club is neon lit, smoky and loud, with a uniform bass beat that sends shock waves through the entire structure.

The Rabbi finds Jimmy in the VIP lounge upstairs. He is smoking a cigarette, watching the people on the dance floor below. A brief nod acknowledges the Rabbi.

"What have you got?" he says. He waves his hand and the room empties of people, fast. The Rabbi sits down.

"I have need of your talents," he says. It's almost a tradition.

"Something big?"

"The blood bank." The Rabbi notices the fleeing reaction of the vampire and knows the bait was taken.

"Impossible."

"No," the Rabbi says. He smiles at the tall vampire. "Just very, very dangerous."

The vampire lights up another cigarette. "How much?" he says finally.

"As much as you can carry."

The Rabbi stands up. "Meet me at the warehouse tomorrow, eight o'clock. Don't be late."

His steps follow the beat as he walks out.

BLUEPRINTS

A dirty moon casts a pale reflection in the river. The warehouse is a low building squatting on a deserted quay. It casts a low reflection in the water.

Naked neon bulbs illuminate the warehouse from within. The Rabbi and his accomplices are standing around a high table.

"Holy water sprinklers?" The Rat is impressed.

"Inconsequential." The Tzaddik is pacing around the room, hands clasped behind his back. "We won't be getting in that way again." He points to the sketch on the table. "The doors are here, here and here. Can they be opened?"

The Rabbi shakes his head. "They're never used, and as far as we know they are purely for show. Ceremonial purpose, if you prefer."

"How does stuff go in and out then?" says Jimmy.

"Exactly," the Rabbi says. He pulls out a different map and lays it gently on the table. "This is an estimate scan of the underground area around the bank. As you can see, there are apparent waste chutes here and here—" he taps the paper "—tunnels here, and possible entry holes here." He pulls out a third map and points to two back alleys some distance from the bank.

"So we get in through the tunnels," says Jimmy the Rat. His cigarette sends curls of grey smoke blowing against the naked bulbs.

"Not exactly," the Rabbi says. "But I want you to check them if you can."

The Rat smiles, fangs shining. "No problem." He stalks out, and at a nod from the Rabbi the Tzaddik follows.

TUNNELS

Jimmy the Rat shape-shifts in the dark alley. Expensive clothes are left in a clatter on the pavement as a long-snout rodent disappears into a crack in the stonework. It moves quickly through the stench of standing water, through a maze of rusting pipes and muddy concrete.

The Tzaddik is standing, wrapped in shadow, in a corner overlooking the bank. The bank's doors are shut. And no light shows through its steel façade.

There is a group of protesters huddled together in the square, holding placards. Free Trade Equals Free Blood, says one. Vampires Are People Too, says another. The Tzaddik silently watches.

Down the pipes the rat runs. Deeper and deeper into the ground, and cautiously edging its way towards the centre. It can smell trouble.

It stops and sniffs the air. Engine oil and wax. It feels small vibrations in the pipe, hears a rhythm of motion coming closer, feels tiny puffs of warm air on its fur.

It moves further down the pipe and emerges into a large, artificially lit tunnel. Unlike the pipes, this tunnel smells clean and efficient, and is hot.

The rat's tail twitches as his head moves rapidly from side to side.

STOP UNFAIR TRADE! screams a sign. FEED THE HUNGRY.

The protesters huddle closer as if the silence of the bank were physically hurting them.

The Tzaddik notices this with interest.

The Rat's small mind is confused. Long-buried memories surface uneasily, of other tunnels, dug in the frozen earth, and of the smells of dead people and human refuse intermingled. Sensing something is wrong, it jumps frantically on a loose pipeline and runs away as fast as its feet can take it.

Behind it, the sound of engines grows louder.

BLUEPRINTS II

"Ultrasonic whistles." The Tzaddik is warming his hands by a large fire. Goldie stands motionless by the door.

"That's what it was?" The Rat is flushed, his skin glistening in the naked light. "Felt it down in the tunnels." He looks over the scattered maps and traces a pattern with his finger. His nails are bitten. "This is roughly the security perimeter. From what I saw there is at least one tunnel large enough to provide transportation, probably several." He draws a vertical line in the air. "I think there's a large shaft here, right under the tower."

"So all the transportation, all personnel going in and out of the bank, do so by means of an underground facility." The Rabbi paces the room, hands locked behind his back. "Good, good."

"Good?" The Rat's fist hits the table, sending papers falling to the floor. "How do you propose we get inside? Turn to rats and slide down the fucking toilet pipes?" He pulls a packet of cigarettes from his shirt and shakes one out. The Tzaddik is quietly collecting the fallen papers and laying them neatly on the table. "It can't be done."

The Rabbi smiles. "Have faith, Jimmy. A man must have faith." He turns to the Tzaddik. "Isn't that right Frankie?"

The Tzaddik's solemn nod doesn't quite hide a sudden smile. "Amen, Rabbi," he says. "Amen."

INTERLUDE II

Somewhere, a phone rings. A large, hairy hand picks up the receiver. A Chopin concerto is playing loudly in the background.

"Yes?" The man is watching the sun setting over the city, painting the skyline in hues of burgundy and crimson as if the fading light were slowly congealing blood.

"They've put the plan into motion."

The man watches an aeroplane flying sedately across the skies, twin jet plumes dispersing in the distance. "Good."

The plane disappears from his field of vision. In the dying skies the smoke remains.

"Jiminy?"

"Yes?" The voice on the other side of the line is strained.

"I hope they don't fuck up."

IMPLEMENTATION

The queues are long and orderly.

In the semi-darkness of dusk the town hall looks obscene, a gothic offence squatting like a bulging toad in a pool of murky light. Security personnel walk up and down the files of people. The guns they hold are unremarkable, meant for efficiency rather than show, the light from street lamps glancing off dull bullet-proof vests.

The queues move slowly, men and women shuffling up the stone stairs and through the great doors. A vast man-like statue stands unobtrusively to one side.

"Next!" A man in a bland, white uniform paces the entrance, clutching a large clipboard. His small moustache is neat. He helps an old woman climb the last step and walks her into the hall, holding her by the arm.

The queues move sluggishly in and out of the building's mouth. On the far side of the plaza, a rat turns into a man in a pool of darkness.

"Did you find it?" The Rabbi is sitting on a wooden bench, his legs stretched.

"Yeah." The Rat is putting on clothes rapidly. "The pipes expand quickly past the back of the hall." He finishes a last button on his shirt, digs in the pocket for a packet of cigarettes. "I think we found your entrance point."

"Good."

The Rat sits down on the bench and draws on his cigarette, cupping the small flame in his hand.

"Now we wait."

* * *

On the stone steps the man with the clipboard looks tired. A deep darkness has fallen, and the plaza in front of the town hall is nearly deserted. He helps an old man—the last in the queue—with the remaining few steps, steadies him as the man seems to overbalance. They walk into the hall together.

Inside, a row of cheap desks lines the spacious room. Behind the desks, men and women in uniforms are helping the last few customers. The guards are all inside, having abandoned the quiet square for the warmer interior. They sit companionably at a large table by the wall, drinking coffee and chatting.

The old man makes his way on his own to the end of the row. A woman, her once-crisp shirt now wrinkled and spotting ugly red smudges, motions for him to sit down.

"Uncuff your shirt please, sir," she says. The old man hesitates, then pulls back his sleeve, revealing a hairless, wiry arm.

"Won't take a moment, sir," the woman says. She dabs a cotton ball on his arm, then reaches for a syringe.

"Will it hurt?" the man asks hesitantly. He scratches a faint scar on his arm.

"A little."

The old man smiles. "Good."

"I'm sorry?" The woman stops, uncertain, the needle raised in the air like a spear.

"Don't be." The old man grabs her and pulls her roughly to the floor, covering her body with his. As he does so, the west wall disappears in a cloud of smoke, knocking down the sitting security guards. In the explosion, giant shards of ancient masonry come flying across the room like a nest of angry wasps, making buzzing sounds in their flight.

Goldie steps through the hole. His feet make no sound as he locates the remaining guards. His movements are slow and precise, and he disposes of the soft human bodies as if conserving both energy and waste, smashing titanium fists on heads that explode silently, leaving crop-circles of blood on the stone floors.

The old man is watching without expression over the prone body of his nurse. He follows the running figures of escaping white uniforms with his eyes as they run through the massive doors and are swallowed by the darkness outside.

Soon there is only silence.

HIJACKING

The Rat steps into the hall, the Rabbi behind him. His face is flushed, the lines bloated and red. Dark sweat glistens on his skin.

"The perimeter," the Rabbi announces, "is clear."

The Tzaddik stands up, pulling the nurse up with him. "Where's the entry point?"

"At the back. Goldie!" At the Rabbi's command the giant golem lumbers to the back of the hall. His fist knocks a hole in the wall, revealing a smooth, metallic pathway sloping downwards.

"Listen carefully." The Tzaddik's eyes hold the frightened nurse motionless, like a snake, or a snake-charmer.

His tone is surprisingly gentle. "We need to get to the bank, and we need your help in doing that. Yes?" He waits until she nods, then continues. "Where we go from here is up to you. Help us, and you'll be home safe in a few hours. Yes?" Again, a nod. "Good. If you choose not to assist my colleagues and myself, or, God forbid, you try to trick us—well, you've seen what Goldie does to people he doesn't like. Yes?"

The nurse nods. Her pupils are enormous dark circles drowning in a milky ocean. The Tzaddik pats her hand. "Good," he says. "Show us how to get to the tower."

The Tzaddik and the nurse walk down the metal passageway. The Rabbi and Jimmy follow. Goldie brings up the rear. There are no lights.

They reach a cul-de-sac, and the Tzaddik propels the nurse forward. Her fingers dance on a small keypad buried in the wall, and a door opens silently, admitting them into a lit tunnel. They stand on a large platform, along which giant vats stand placidly, filled with a ruby-coloured liquid. There is no sound in the tunnel.

Beside the platform a bullet-shaped train stands idle. At the Tzaddik's direction the nurse punches another code into another keypad, this time embedded in the dull casing of the train, and its doors open quietly.

"Jimmy, Goldie, check the train." The Rabbi's voice echoes, distorted, in the soundless tunnel.

"Empty."

"Tzaddik?"

His voice is barely more than a hiss. "Be quiet." The

Tzaddik is standing by the entrance, his face blanked. In the silence, the cause of his concern becomes evident.

There are shuffling sounds emanating from the narrow tunnel they have just vacated.

CRIMINAL OFFENCE

The door to the tunnel comes crashing down, nearly burying the Tzaddik under its weight.

"What the…"

A progression of bodies appears in the doorway, moving slowly forward. At the head of the line is a body in a once-white smock, its head a pulp of gristle. It reaches scarred hands to the Tzaddik and pulls him forward, engulfing him in a hug of iron that threatens to snap his spine. Behind him, other mutilated bodies enter and spread across the platform, walking blindly toward the living.

The nurse is swallowed up by a horde of bodies. Her head tumbles to the floor and lies still, eyes staring vacantly into space.

"Goddamn the bank." The Rabbi's voice is taut, angry. "Raising the dead is a criminal offence!"

He pulls a long strip of cloth out of his pocket, unfolding it to reveal various wood- and metal-etched symbols.

"Help Frankie while I do this!" he shouts to the Rat, who is already moving, jumping on the mutilated zombie from behind. He sinks his teeth into the zombie's neck and takes a savage bite that leaves the head hanging. The zombie drops the Tzaddik and turns around to face the Rat, who is moving again, running at the ruined bodies of their attackers like a rabid dog.

Goldie disposes of two of the attackers, hugging them tightly before biting their heads off with his metallic teeth. The bodies hiss when his teeth touch skin, and he throws the remains onto the tracks before progressing to more advancing zombies.

The Rabbi's hands are dancing across the cloth, picking and throwing objects. More zombies drop to the floor, truly dead, as a cascade of crosses, stars of David, mandalas and swastikas cut through their skin with their jagged edges. Smoke hisses each time a particular symbol corresponds to a zombie's weakness.

Soon the platform is filled with bodies.

"They keep coming!" The Rat's teeth are bloody, their colouring unhealthy. "We've got to get out of here."

"Into the train. Quickly." The Rabbi throws his last weapon, a silver cross that penetrates to the heart of an approaching zombie, and walks quickly towards the train. "Hold them, Goldie."

The Rat joins him, the Tzaddik staggering alongside. "Can you drive this thing?"

"I can." The Tzaddik enters the driver's side, kicking a lumbering zombie viciously in the face, crunching its nose bone. "Ready?"

The Rabbi calls Goldie, who is standing almost motionless on the platform, dispatching approaching bodies with the minimum of movement. His sleek body is covered in red hues as if illegible graffiti had been sprayed on him for too long.

"Ready."

"Then let's get the fuck out of here!" The Tzaddik hits buttons rapidly with one hand. As the doors close, he throws a small bundle out of the window and onto the platform.

As the train disappears into the dark tunnel, the platform behind them erupts in flame and once-human bodies topple and burn silently until they are lost from view.

UP

The heart of the tower is a cold darkness. Frost clumps the walls like persistent moss.

The train pulls silently to a stop in a dimly-lit terminal. Its passengers dislodge carefully.

"So *nu*?" the Tzaddik says. "Where do we go from here?"

The Rat is scanning the walls. "An elevator shaft," he announces. He looks hungrily around him. On the terminal, rows of neatly lined barrels shine wetly.

"Leave the blood," the Rabbi orders, "I want the whole thing, not just a batch." He walks to the elevator and punches the call button. The doors open without a sound.

They pile in, standing side by side, and the Rabbi presses the top button.

"We're in."

"Let's not hang around *too* long, okay?"

"One thing at a time," the Rabbi says. "One thing at a time."

* * *

The doors open onto an empty corridor. To their left is a small window and when they glance through it they can see the city sprawled underneath, a maze of lights far below.

"This must be how the previous burglar got in," the Tzaddik comments.

"Which means we can probably expect some rain soon." The Rat smiles, sharp teeth gleaming.

They walk down the corridor, reach an unmarked door. The Tzaddik tries the handle, then bends down to the lock with a couple of narrow metal bars.

"Very old fashioned." He opens the door and they go through.

"*A werehouse.*"

"Stands to reason."

They are in a vast room, a *werehouse* filled from floor to ceiling with giant vats in which a red liquid swirls and spins.

"Jackpot," The Rat breathes.

"Indeed." The Rabbi surveys the room. "Where is the control room?"

The Tzaddik and the golem walk to the other end of the room, where another unmarked door is set.

"Goldie?" The Tzaddik motions with his hand. The golem, almost gently, pushes the door until it comes off the hinges and falls to the floor with a loud bang.

Then, almost as gently, he disintegrates.

DÉNOUEMENT

A heap of fine powder lies on the floor where Goldie has been. Light emanates through the doorway, illuminating the large werehouse as if by bouts of lightning.

"What can kill a golem?" the Tzaddik's voice is low in the silence.

"*The question is who.*"

A figure materialises in the doorway, a glowing, human-shaped apparition, casting light around it in a concentrated halo.

"*Tzaddik.*" The figure's voice echoes through their heads, the silent sound of distant thunder.

"Fallen One." The Tzaddik's face is impassive.

"*It's been a while, Angel Killer.*"

"Not long enough."

"*In that I agree.*"

The Rat and the Rabbi stand back, their bodies and faces frozen.

"What are you doing here, Angel?"

"*Dealing...*" The angel's laugh is like a bass beat. "*Wheeling...and dealing.*"

"In blood?"

"*Such a common commodity. And yet, so useful.*" Youthful lips curl into a tight smile. "*I like my job.*"

The Tzaddik smiles as well, and his smile is unpleasant. "That's a shame," he says. "Because you're fired." He utters a short sentence, half-bark and half-song, and the silence snaps.

The blood vats explode.

"Down down *down!*" The Tzaddik shouts, and the Rabbi and Jimmy duck as the spell is broken, lying flat on the floor as blood comes pouring over the werehouse like a red storm, flowing and raging in great sheets of crimson rain.

The werehouse is a raging ocean of blood

The angel rages, but shrinks in fear as the blood comes pouring towards him, his light diminishing as the red liquid touches his feet.

"Never send an angel to do a man's job." The Tzaddik voice is raw.

"You'll die one day, angel killer. Even Eternal Wanderings must come to an end." The angel's face is a mask of hatred. *"And I will be there when it happens."*

As the blood pushes into the room, the light is dimming fast. Soon, the room is once more in semi-darkness as the angel fades away, a broken vessel brimming with an endless supply of spilled blood.

"Did you have to waste all that blood?" the Rabbi says. "Never mind. Help me with Jimmy, I think he's had more than is good for him."

They carry the bloated figure of the vampire on their shoulders and wade out of the room.

"I'm sorry about your golem."

"Thank you," the Rabbi says. "I'll miss him."

"What do we do now?"

"Contact that officious gentleman who is paying our bill, give him the keys to the bank and split with the cash." The Rabbi glances at the Tzaddik. "What will you do with the money?"

The Tzaddik smiles, shrugs.

"Go on holiday," he says. "A *long* holiday."

They walk down the corridor, two old men and a vampire, and the darkness swallows them whole.

TRANSYLVANIAN MISSION

This story was much inspired by my own family's history in Transylvania and the terrible fate that was to befall many of them with the late Nazi invasion into Hungary. I used my own visit to that remote region—in the summer of 1994—as inspiration, when bullet holes could still be seen in the walls from the violent overthrow of Nicolae Ceaușescu. The other influence is, of course, *Dracula*—as well as the historical personage who was Vlad Tepes, or "The Impaler." The castle itself is a rather pleasant building when visited on a bright summer's day, and lies not too far from Brașov.

CARPATHIAN MOUNTAINS, MAY 1944

It was an old man's war, the Rat thought for the hundredth time.

He surveyed the despondent group of aged troops and sighed. Spread on the damp ground the partisans sat, huddled each into themselves. Stars shone with a pale, sickly light over the thick canopy of trees. The Allies Recon officer was standing to one side, shaving blindly, swearing in a mixture of languages each time he cut himself. The Rat smelled the blood, tasting it on his tongue. The Englishman was an unnecessary complication.

He shrugged and went back to his book, a small, hardbound English edition of Bram Stoker's *Dracula*, and continued to struggle with the uncomfortable language. Naturally, or rather, *unnaturally* he thought with a trace of amusement, he had no problem reading the book in what his troops would consider near total darkness. The irony of that, and of reading this book in particular, did not escape him.

They were waiting, the small group of Jewish refugees, had been waiting for so long that they had lost all thought of victory. The old and the infirm, the invalid and the mad, left behind while their families and friends were carted off by train to far-away Poland and killed, as efficiently and as coldly as a rat-catcher disposed of rats. Now, they took refuge in the mountain terrain of the Carpathians, hiding on the Romanian side of the border, spending what time they had left in puny raids against the Germans that seemed to have no effect... no effect at all. The last Recon officer, another unpleasant Englishman—Malory, his name was—was quite scathing about it. They found him one morning lying naked in a pool of melted snow. The grass around him was yellow where the group of *iele* had feasted on him during the night. The partisans had put a stake through his heart and left him to rot.

It didn't take long.

There was the sound of a bird hooting in the distance. The Rat put the book away and stood up, waiting. A minute later, young Pèter burst into the clearing, his misshapen face excited. Without expression, the Rat gave him a bottle of wine and waited while the boy drank.

"Report?" he asked at last, seeing that Pèter's breathing had settled.

The boy was the only one left of his family. He had been saved by an old neighbour who had kept him on his isolated farm, and made to work at the pens and the house and later, at night, in the old man's bed. For all that, he had retained an innocence that owed, the Rat thought, more to his deformed birth than to reality, yet for all that was still touching, still somehow noble. It was best, the Rat sometimes thought, if all the children of the age were born simple, so that they wouldn't know it when the Nazis took them, when the showers opened up and Zyklon-B came pouring out instead of water.

Pèter's usually cheerful countenance showed excitement. "T-there are p-people coming," he announced. "F-from across the b-border. Here," he thrust a crumpled piece of paper into the Rat's hand, gazing up at him, complete trust in his eyes. "F-from Lalo."

The Rat opened the paper, motioning for the kid to sit himself down. Someone passed Pèter bread, and he sat munching at it happily.

The Rat scanned the note, his interest quickening. He motioned for the Englishman. "What do you think?" he asked, passing him the note. The Englishman fumbled for matches, cursed as he lit one and cupped it protectively in his hand.

He read the note and shrugged. "Worth a look?" he suggested, his put-upon drawl negating the words.

His reaction was interesting, the Rat thought. Very casual. Very...*nonchalant*. "Was there anything about this from HQ?"

The Englishman shrugged again. "Not a word."

The Rat didn't like it. There were not many people coming across the border from occupied Hungary, even though the Romanian government was allied with the Nazis. For anyone to make the trip to this remote location, the reason had to be important. He didn't like the implications of that.

His little group of partisans, assembled as much by loss as by any real desire to inflict damage on the Germans, did not make a very strong strike force, he was the first to admit. The aged and the infirm and the sick—it was, he thought yet again, an old man's war they had stumbled into.

Nevertheless, he motioned for his troops to prepare for movement.

* * *

Nestled between mountain ranges, the city of Brasov lay like a sparkling jewel amidst the darkness of the Carpathians. Pinpricks of light burned like a promise of tranquility. Here, there were still Jews.

The partisans were arranged in a crescent moon high

above the road leading into the city from Sighisoara and beyond, from Nazi-occupied Hungary. They waited in silence.

The Rat crouched, his senses alert. There was blood on the wind again, old, sick blood, and something else that was less familiar. A musky scent, animal-like and threatening. Like a *strigoi*, he thought suddenly, remembering the rare times he had run into one of their kin, roaming the mountains in the guise of a wolf or a dog.

But there had been none that he knew of for at least a hundred years. Whatever this smell was, it was not local, not part of the unnatural fauna of Transylvania.

He quieted the sense of unease and settled himself to wait. Lalo's note was ambiguous, uncertain, his handwriting jutting over the page like the handiwork of a crazed spider. *People are coming,* was all it said. *From across the border. Watch for them on the way to Brasov.*

Even committing this much to paper was dangerous. Whoever was coming must have been important, to warrant a note. They all liked Pèter, but sometimes, if you wanted to make sure...

There were faint sounds on the wind, growing in volume as they came near. Jeeps, he thought. Two, maybe three. Scents of gasoline—gasoline and gunpowder. And the heavy musk of some feral animal, one that fed on rotting meat and corpses.

The Rat spat quietly and suddenly grinned, his elongated fangs slicing the night air. Nazis. He could smell them, coming nearer.

The sound of car engines grew louder. Soon, they could see beams of light moving nearer, wavering wildly on the dirt road. The partisans cowered into the ground, feeling a sudden fear like a physical object hurling at them from the moving jeeps. The Rat burrowed deeper into the shadows, his face contorting in sudden rage.

Like *strigoi*. He glanced at the Englishman, saw him fingering the small silver cross at his neck. He knew what they were.

The Rat filed the information away and watched. *Two, three, four jeeps. One large truck, ambling like a drunkard below. Machine guns, one for every jeep.* They moved in a protective formation, two jeeps in the front, two at the rear, guarding the truck. *Someone, or some thing, important in there*, he thought. He watched, recording the scene in his mind, noting the number of indistinct shapes in the open jeeps, estimating military capacity, finding potential weak spots. The fact that he couldn't see the figures clearly bothered him. Like *strigoi*. The thought hammered at him insistently. Like dogs. Like wolves. There were rumours...

Directly underneath them, the convoy suddenly stopped. The shapes in the jeeps shifted, blurred faces looking up, scanning the horizon.

The partisans shrunk even deeper into the embrace of the dark.

The Rat held his breath, but their position was faultless: high, secure, and—as far the convoy below was concerned—ineffective. They were strictly observers—for now.

As if satisfied of that, sensing that what had disturbed them was not an immediate threat, the jeep engines started again, and the convoy slowly passed from view, disappearing at last into the gates of Brasov.

The Rat sidled close to the Englishman, who was crouching low in the surrounding shrubs, a little way away from the partisans, as if their presence made him uncomfortable. "What were those things?" he asked conversationally, his voice low.

The Englishman spat on the ground, his hand still fingering the cross on his neck. "What do you think?"

In answer, the Rat moved.

Elongated fingers, their nails stretched and sharpened like unpolished knives, moved with lightning speed and grabbed the officer by the throat. The Rat lifted the Englishman in the air, slamming him against a nearby tree, and held him there, choking, a foot above the earth. "I *don't* think," the Rat said.

Around them, the silence was even more pronounced than before as each partisan studiously avoided taking any notice of the scene taking place.

"Now, why don't you tell me what the fuck those *things* were, and why you don't seem very surprised to see them here? And perhaps, if you would be so kind, you could fill me in on what HQ *does* have to say about this little nightly excursion?"

He could feel his fangs protruding, hurting his jaw, see the effect of the raw smell of his breath, like dry, old blood, on the suffocating Englishman. He had to feed, soon. He only wished it could be now, this place, this person.

With regret, he loosened his grip and the English-man fell to the floor, his hands around his neck. He was breathing heavily, making wheezing, choked sounds.

"So *nu*," the Rat said at last. "What do you know?"

* * *

The night was coming slowly to an end. The Rat moved like a shadow through the dark, cobbled streets of Bra-sov, a deeper darkness that seemed to suck starlight, and the occasional illumination of a lamp carried drunkenly down narrow alleyways.

He waited.

Lengthened nails and fangs like needles, and coarse dark hair accumulating like fine dust over his frame. Hunger.

Hunger and, at the back of the mind, apprehension. He was worried, worried about the thing the English-man had said.

"They're fucking werewolves," he had said at last, mas-saging his bruised neck. "The Gestapo's very own *Wolf-kommando*. HQ said a whole unit of them was ordered to Berlin two weeks ago. At the express orders of the Führer."

He stopped, drawing air desperately into his lungs. The look he gave the Rat was, incredibly, a look of reproach, as if he were merely disappointed with the ungentlemanly behaviour of this uncouth field officer.

Like the last one, the Rat thought grimly. The Allied

officers simply refused to acknowledge anything that smacked of the supernatural, and that, quite frankly, made them a liability. It made them careless.

He remembered the one before Malory. An Armenian man, ex-Air Force. He wasn't so bad, just wanted to get out of the war any way he could.

The mound of earth where they had buried him, deep in the mountains, testified to the way his final escape had come about.

The Rat waited. The residents of Brasov were not as sceptical. Crosses hung in windows, on doors. Bunches of garlic dangled from window-frames, unobtrusively.

He grimaced. The crosses, naturally, didn't bother him, but the garlic was unpleasant. No one, of course, was fool enough to put silver where it could be stolen.

Finally, noise reached him. The figure of a man lurched on the road, bottle in hand. He was muttering to himself. Large frame, but unsteady. Good. Probably a farmer on a night in the town.

He waited until the man was passing right by him, almost touching the shadow that was the Rat, and attacked.

And was pushed against the wall with inhuman strength, the bottle smashing against his face, spraying him with shards of sharp, painful glass.

A trap. He ducked a second punch and drove his razor-like nails into the man's abdomen, hard, moving up in a bloody arc through his body, opening a large, gaping gash.

The man screamed, a high, keening howl that turned into a low growl of rage. His body shifted impossibly in the starlight, coarse, hard fur growing over his skin, his frame changing, hands becoming large, threatening forelegs.

Large, wet teeth bit at the Rat's leg. He kicked, connected, and as the wolf howled again flew at it, sinking fangs into its belly.

It was not a pretty sight, not the gentle bleeding of a man or woman as they stood unresisting, trapped against him. This time was different: a feeding frenzy against a dying, dangerous animal. He stooped by the side of the wolf, crouching in a growing pool of blood, and fed, like an animal himself. Organs torn out and discarded on the pavement, bones cracked and broken by his probing fingers, and the blood, the blood flowing into him, something between animal and man, blood that came gushing and gushing out.

When he was finished, it was nearly dawn. The sun sent pale fingers against the horizon like the promise of an iron fist. He had to leave.

At his feet, the corpse of a young-looking man lay like a deflated doll.

* * *

The Nazis departed the next day. Of the dead soldier there was no mention.

The Rat guessed they preferred to keep their journey, and the nature of the soldiery itself, quiet. It was not long ago that Germany had officially invaded Hungary, and there was talk now that the days of the Iron Guard were soon to be over, and that Romania should join the Allies. Dangerous talk, for the moment, but the reality was that the Nazis were becoming less than welcome.

They did not, however, go far.

It was late evening the next day. The Rat crouched low behind a boulder, observing the little camp the *Wolf-kommando* had established in the common underneath the castle. Two small fires burned between vehicles and tents, arranged in a protective square. Of all the figures moving in the dark, only one man was clear to his vision. The rest, the *werewolves*, were blurred, as if light bent itself around them in strange, confusing angles. The man was young and fit-looking, dressed in the uniform of a senior officer. In his hand he held a riding crop which he was tapping methodically against his boots.

They were, the Rat thought, waiting for something.

He motioned to Lalo, the Hungarian Resistance's contact person with the Jewish partisans. He had shown up shortly after his delivered note but remained stubbornly reticent with further information.

The Rat suspected that, in honesty, Lalo simply didn't know. He was there representing the concerns of the Hungarians, whose channels of information were limited. The arrival of the Nazi troops left them worried.

Understandably.

"What do you think they're up to?" the Rat asked, nevertheless.

Lalo spat carefully on the ground and made the sign of the cross in the air. The lines of his face were pronounced, etched in deeper grooves than before.

The man was afraid.

"*Dracul.*" He said the word like a curse.

The Rat grimaced as the man once again spat ritually on the ground and made the sign of the cross. *Fucking peasants.*

"Don't be an idiot," he said at last, still watching the Nazis. "No devils, at least not apart from the one right in front of us."

The German officer was preparing something. Curious tools, medical implements of polished metal, gleamed in the firelight. The wolves were also moving now, checking weapons, talking in low voices that did not carry over to where Lalo and the Rat hid. Nevertheless, the feeling of expectation was tangible.

They were preparing to move.

The Rat made his decision. "Lalo, go back to camp," he said. "Bring some of the boys over to keep an eye on them during the night."

"And you, Rat?" Lalo's face betrayed a mixture of his suspicion and relief. He didn't trust him, the Rat knew, just as he, in turn, did not trust Lalo and his masters. Yet the man's relief at leaving this place was tangible.

"I'll stay here." His eyes had not left the German officer. "I want to see where they're going."

He waited until the Hungarian left, disappearing into the dark forest like a wild cat, leaving barely a footprint in his passage. He was good, the Rat had to give him that.

He waited.

After fifteen minutes, the Nazis were apparently ready. At the command of their officer they began to march, assuming the same formation they did with their vehicles. From afar, it looked unnatural, the man surrounded on all sides by blurred figures, as if he walked in a circle of darkness. They began to move up the hill, toward the castle.

Bran Castle stood like a fairy tale mirage, failing completely, in the Rat's opinion, to look the part of a sinister dwelling. It was built by knights of the Teutonic Order over seven centuries before, and its main claim to fame was its temporary occupancy, in the 15th century, by the Impaler. Now, it was supposed to be occupied by members of the royal family. The Queen, it was said, was exiled by her husband King Carol, who had found himself enchanted by a new mistress—a Jewish one, no less. Others said it was Princess Ileana who lived there, fleeing Hungary from the Nazis.

It didn't, however, appear to be currently occupied.

The Rat hurried like a shadow along the cliff wall, the light of a near-full moon sending a shiver of apprehension down his spine as he thought of the *Wolfkommando* ascending to the same place.

Castle Dracul. Devil's castle.

The Rat climbed in the shadow of Mount Bucegi to the castle. There was a gun-hole there, a narrow shaft through which arrows would have once been shot.

With distaste, he changed.

A rat climbed through the narrow shaft and entered the castle.

A vampire stalked Bran Castle once more.

At least, if the old stories were in fact true. The Rat remembered Tepes vaguely, a petty tyrant like so many of the ones before him and after. Impaler, yes, but no kind of *strigoi* the Rat had ever seen.

He lived, briefly, and he died. And that was that.

Until now.

He changed back, hauling his clothes through the narrow gun shaft, dressing in silence.

He was inside a walled court that was open to the stars. The castle rose above him, looking, he thought, more homey than foreboding, a rather comfortable, solid structure. There were flowers in the courtyard, and a tree.

He moved cautiously forward, entering a small room that appeared to be a chapel. A basin of holy water stood by the wall, and he dipped his hand in it, flicking the water against the wall, wondering for the hundredth time why some of his kind found the substance—no different from regular water, as far as he could tell—to be so deadly.

There were sounds coming from above. The Nazis were in the castle.

The Rat felt suddenly uneasy, as if the presence of the Nazis, somehow, had disturbed the castle, was slowly awaking something old and rather unpleasant.

Nonsense.

He followed the source of the noise.

"We must find the crypt," a voice said sharply in the dark. It was the officer.

"We will, Herr Mengale," a second voice answered, a hint of amusement in its tone. "We will."

Mengale. That was Mengale, the butcher of Auschwitz. The name echoed in the Rat's ears. He felt blood thirst consuming him, a burning flame of anger and hate that threatened to take control of him.

He stilled with an effort, breathing slowly.

"Search the castle, look for hidden pathways. Be extremely cautious. He must still be alive!" His voice shook in sudden passion. "And he killed one of you, as if Moritz was nothing but a chicken to be plucked." The staccato beat of his riding crop increased. *They must think it was* Tepes *who killed their boy in Brasov!* The thought made him grin, and his tongue ran alongside his teeth, like a soldier checking his weapons.

The Rat climbed cautiously up to the second floor, catching sight of the German in the distance, standing by a suit of armour. "We must find him." Mengale's eyes had an unnatural glow in the dark. "Find him, and bring him over to the Reich."

"Do you hear that, *Dracul?*" he suddenly shouted. "I could make you the prince of this little land again!"

There was no answer, yet the hairs on the Rat's arms stood suddenly, the second time in so many minutes. So this was what the Nazis were about. He should have

guessed. Hitler must have found the old Impaler prac-
tically *inspiring*.

Idiots.

He slid alongside the walls, giving the German a wide
berth. Only two soldiers were in the room with him,
and they were occupied. He entered another chapel, a
room made up in old-fashioned, gothic architecture.
More holy water.

This place, in a way, had quite high security. He wondered why.

"Herr Mengale!" The sudden shout echoed, distorted,
against the cold stone walls. "We've found a hidden
staircase."

The beat of boots against flagstones sounded rapidly.
He followed at a distance. The soldiers, he saw, had
hacked away at the wall, exposing a large passage lined
with stairs heading upward.

Mengale's riding crop made rapid rhythms against his
boots.

"See what's up there," he said.

Two of the soldiers hurried into the passageway. The
Rat retreated to his original position and used the stairs.

Everything was going according to plan.

He climbed up to the second floor. No sign of the
soldiers. Third.

Fourth.

He paused.

As battles went, the Rat later had to admit to himself,
this one was something of a farce.

A room. A darkness that was more than the absence of light. He stepped cautiously, sliding along the wall, his every sense alert.

And was blinded by the sudden glare of an electric lamp, the powerful projector catching him like a stag in the glare of a jeep.

Trapped.

Three shadows, cornering him.

Blurred.

Werewolves.

He lashed out, met no resistance, overbalanced. Blind, he was helpless. He didn't dare to change his shape.

Not in the presence of three big fucking dogs.

Still, he made to run.

It could have worked. A quick dive through the window and he'd be flying down the cliff, away from the castle. It would have hurt, but he would have survived.

It didn't happen.

He felt a sharp jab in his back, and the world went black.

* * *

It was some time later.

"Tell me about…Dracula," Dr. Mengale said patiently.

His voice was surprisingly pleasant, yet it was offset disconcertingly by the staccato sound of his riding crop tapping against the dark leather riding boots he wore.

The Rat grinned through bloodied lips. The Nazis had strapped him into a metal chair that felt cold and strangely slimy against his skin. They had bound him meticulously. Wires, in which iron was woven with fine strands of silver and gold, held his legs and his arms. And through the wires, like a whisper of death, came the faintest touch of raw electricity. It was, for now, only a tingle in his flesh, but the implications were obvious.

"Dracula?" Dr. Mengale prompted. The riding crop taps went just a fraction faster.

The Rat mentally shrugged.

"Well," he said. He adopted the didactic voice the one-before-last Allies Recon officer had often used. In guttural German it sounded strange. "It is essentially a love story, taking its cue from both the travel novel and, to an extent, the English pornographic tradition that starts with Fanny Hill…"

FLASH.

The Rat had known pain. Pain, after all, was a part of life, and in a life, or at least an undeath as long as his—metaphysics wasn't really his field—there was pain in plenitude. The Rat screamed as the current shot through his bloodied body, his figure metamorphosing wildly in the agony as his mind lost control, became subsumed by the all-encompassing pain. The wires, like living, serpentine things, shrunk and expanded along with his changing body, keeping him bound.

Then it was gone, as if someone simply pressed a button labelled pain.

Which, he realised when his mind came back to his body, was exactly what happened. It was what he had found most scary about Mengale, he suddenly understood. Every other person would have threatened him with exposure to the sun, with holy symbols, religious iconography, even—as Tepes was fond of doing to his enemies—impaling him through the rear, a particularly unpleasant method that would have kept even a mortal man alive for several hours, and the rat undoubtedly longer. But those methods were not for Mengale. For him, the process had to be clinical and precise, a measured, scientific way of inflicting the most amount of pain with the least amount of mess and fuss.

The Rat coughed and let blood dribble through his exposed fangs onto his shirt. As much as he wanted to, he wouldn't risk spitting at the Doctor. It was too soon after the pain, and he needed the blood.

"I concede your point," Mengale said affably. The riding crop was again doling out measured beats. "Dracula is a literary construction. Well done." He smiled and, in the entry to the tent, the two *Wolfkommando* smiled as well, exposing large, sharp teeth that glinted dull in the electric light.

"Tell me about Tepes." Mengale's voice changed when he said the name. "Did he…turn you?"

It was eagerness, the Rat realised. Mengale was fascinated with Tepes, fascinated with the Rat. And he knew, with a cold, hard certainty, that he had to escape, escape quickly, or he would become yet another subject for Mengale's dissections, his research.

"No," he said at last. Mengale waited. "Vlad Tepes was

just a man. Honourable, as far it went, a good Christian. He was no *Pricolici*."

FLASH.

"You lie." Mengale's voice came faint through the torrents of pain racking his body. "Where is Tepes?"

"Dead," the Rat whispered. He coughed, more blood, dirty blood, seeping into his lap. "Dead."

FLASH.

"Where is Tepes?" Dr. Mengale's voice was even. "Where is *Herr Dracul*?"

The questioning went long into the night. At times, the Rat was lucky enough to lose consciousness. But it was never for long.

* * *

Sunlight burned against his retinas.

The Rat groaned, tasting crusted blood on his lips. His skin was burning.

He tried to move, found himself unable. He was lying on bare earth, by the feel of it, his hands and legs tied by thick ropes.

The heat was unbearable.

He turned his head to the side and opened his eyes cautiously, ignoring the sudden pain that shot through his brain.

Sunrise.

Over Mount Bucegi the sun was rising, dawn breaking over the Arges valley.

He was going to die.

It was the cruellest way to kill a vampire. The stake, the silver bullet, the potent religious symbols (it was said truly old vampires feared the swastika most of all, the powerful old symbol corrupted by the Nazis. *Of course*, he thought, *nowadays everyone, vampire or not, feared the swastika—with reason*), all these were relatively quick means, means of fear and urgency. This, though…Mengale chose well. It was as if the Impaler had found himself a spiritual heir in this one, another man who knew how to attenuate pain, to stretch out the agony of his victims, making death seem like a blissful release when at last it came.

He tried, desperately, to shapeshift, trying to shrink to the minute figure of a rat. It was no use. He coughed blood and felt his skin begin to blister.

It would be a long, painful death. But then, the Rat thought, it was the way all Jews died, nowadays. Compared to Mengale's test subjects in Auschwitz, his death would be brief, merciful.

He howled in pain and with a sudden anger that threatened to overwhelm him, coursing through his body like fire, like a keg of powder threatening to explode.

The Rat screamed hate to the skies.

In the bowels of Bran Castle Dr. Mengale nodded at the sound, as if acknowledging that an experiment result was satisfying. The *Wolfkommando* digging through the earth in the dank room around him smiled, showing white, elongated teeth.

And in the membrane of the castle, in the old earth

and the brittle bones of stone, in the deep shadows and pure, undiluted dark, something stirred, as if disturbed from slumber.

And in the shadows of the forest the partisans heard, and at last, wary and afraid, they came to his aid.

There was nothing, the Rat later thought—lying buried in the damp ground, surrounded by darkness and silence, recuperating—nothing to bind that group of desperate old men to him. They had no reason to feel love or kinship for him, the *strigoi*, yet they congregated around him, through webs of hate or desperation or shame, and at last they came to him. Those who couldn't save the lives of their loved ones saved his.

He was burning when they reached him, the flames setting the ropes alight, still screaming defiance at the skies. They covered him in thick, heavy cloths, dampening his fire, and cut his bonds, and silenced his shrieks.

There were some men amongst them who knew about those things. They carried him deep into the forest and buried him in a shallow grave, where the trees were thickest and let no sunlight through.

And waited for him.

Immortally wounded, the Rat slept in the Earth. The partisans raided the farms nearby, procuring chickens and pigs, and lay traps in the forest for hares. When the Rat rose, at last, they fed him, dribbling the blood into his gaping mouth, each drop like a precious burgundy-coloured stone falling into a chasm.

The Rat awoke, and he wasn't alone.

All through his journey through the castle, through his torture, pinned up in the killing sun, buried in the earth, he could feel it. Ancient, angry, not human—not *strigoi*, either.

Something had awakened at Castle Bran.

TIRGOVISTE, JULY 1944

There were rumours of impending change. It was there in the hushed conversations of stall-holders in the market square, and in the eyes of the street children. It was there in the faint, coded radio transmissions from underground cells all across Europe. It was everywhere.

The Red Army was coming. The tide of war was turning.

But for the partisans, hope was something that had died long ago, burned away with their families in far away Auschwitz.

High above the old church, the Rat crouched like a gargoyle, blanketed in darkness. Watching.

The Butcher of Auschwitz had not yet left Romania. Radio messages insisted he was back in Poland, back at his experiments, back to supervising the ovens. But the Rat knew differently. The Nazis were still there, still searching, in a manner he could only think of as desperate, for the elusive Tepes. The *Dracul*.

And they had come, finally, to Tirgoviste, the Impaler's ancient capital, for one last attempt to enlist the help of the Führer's imagined hero.

The Rat waited.

Below, Tirgoviste's ancient market square was abandoned. A half-moon, large and misshaped, shone high on the horizon, casting the square in a pale, unearthly light. On the old flagstones, nothing moved.

He waited.

Presently there was the sound of engines in the distance, growing louder. Narrow beams of light materialised as the sound intensified, moving frantically as a row of jeeps—and the now familiar truck—entered the square in formation.

The Rat grinned, tasting the wind with his tongue, running it alongside his elongated fangs. Dogs. They had a special stench. He was looking forward to meeting them again.

The *Wolfkommando* moved out of the jeeps and spread out, guns at the ready. Times were changing, and danger was more palpable now, more conceivable than when they first set out into what had been—still was, officially—friendly territory.

Mengale stepped out of the truck. Behind him came the struggling figure of a young girl, clasped roughly by the arm and dragged along. The Rat's eyes narrowed, but he didn't move.

She was young, he estimated, no more than fifteen. She had the stark, dark beauty of a *Cigani*, a gypsy, and he felt the anger rising in him again, like a tide breaking against rock. It was a miracle there were any gypsies left, any that were not incinerated in the ovens along with the Jews.

Mengale marched her forward, towards the church. The only sound in the square was that of his boots echoing distortedly, not corresponding entirely to his steps. The girl's bare feet made no sound on the flagstones.

She looked frightened.

The Rat felt the hairs on his arms stand on end. It was that same feeling, that same presence he dimly felt at Bran, the one felt in his makeshift grave. *Was it Tepes?* he wondered. There was a lot in Transylvania that remained hidden, even from him.

Perhaps.

Mengale stopped in front of the church. His eyes roved over the building, then seemed to hover, almost stare directly at the point where the Rat was crouched. A smile played on his lips.

"Impaler," Mengale said loudly into the air.

He extracted a long, surgical blade from his jacket. Seeing this, the girl tried to wrench her arm away in panic. He hit her, a backhanded slap that sent her reeling on the flagstones.

"I will make you this sacrifice, in the name of the Führer." He extended his arm in the air, displaying a freshly-laundered armband with a swastika on it. "Heil Dracul!" he shouted.

On cue, the *Wolfkommando* all turned as one to face the church. "Heil Dracul!" they cried, extending their arms in a Nazi salute.

The girl began to cry in loud, gasping sobs that seemed to suck in all the air around her.

The feeling, the presence, that the Rat was feeling intensified. He shifted his gaze, scanning the rooftops, noting the position of his men. They were going to take out the Nazis, no matter what happened.

Mengale's hand came whipping down towards the girl, the blade glinting in the moonlight.

It only took a moment.

The blade cut across her neck, severing her cries, sending blood spouting on to the ancient flagstones. The girl's body collapsed, crashing softly to the ground.

She lay in a pool of blood and Mengale waited, wiping the blade thoroughly on a handkerchief before returning it to his coat pocket.

The handkerchief he dropped, as if in distaste, on top of the body.

In the sudden tension—the feeling of the presence was now overwhelming for the Rat—a wind rose at the entrance to the church. Dust ebbed and flowed in complex patterns that floated and merged, forming eyes, mouths, liquid faces that changed and ran into each other.

The wind formed mouths, some crooked, some bloodied, and spoke through them. It spoke in many voices: in old dialects of Romanian, of Magyar, of Mongol and German. The sound was like a shockwave, sending Mengale reeling, disturbing the corpse so that it rolled, pathetically, on its side.

Even the *Wolfkommando* were affected, crouching low against the bellows of sound and wind, their faces changing, teeth lengthening, rough hair growing uncontrollably.

"*Ordög!*" The sound broke windows, threw carts in the air, intensifying. "*Pokol!*"

From above, the Rat watched, trying to resist the power of the wind. It was trying to force him to change, to mould himself into animal form. To revert to savagery, as it was doing to the Nazis below. His mind fought against the change, watching the metamorphosing faces, conjuring identities for them from the deepest recesses of his mind. There were Boyars there, noblemen and petty kings, princes and bloodied rulers. He saw Tepes' face there, merging into that of a Knight Templar, then into an unfamiliar face with Asiatic features.

They were all there, these ancient men who each fought for Transylvania and for Wallachia, these elder kings who were roused at last from their slumber.

"*Ordög!*" the voices screamed. "*Pokol!*"

The Rat gritted his teeth. *Devil*, the dead kings were shouting, and *Hell*. It was as if they had finally encountered a kind of evil they couldn't understand, a precise and tidy kind, one that didn't gloat over its mutilated victims, but rather sat down to note the fact in volume after volume of leather-bound ledgers.

Fighting the wind, the Rat signalled to his men.

The volley of ancient bullets flew like drunken mosquitoes through the turbulent air, ripping bloodied gashes in the animal hides of the *Wolfkommando*. The Germans roared, howling anger and pain at the skies, at the partisans and the ghosts of the kings, and their howl was a thing of menace and fear intermingled. *It was a tragedy*, the Rat thought, *that the Nazis had managed to subdue even these wild and feral creatures, and mould them in their own image.* They smelled of a corruption that penetrated all the way to the soul.

He prepared to jump. Below, the bellowing wind still fought the wolves—now entirely transformed—while from above, almost unnoticed in the confusion, the partisans rained down their bullets. *If only they had silver*, the Rat thought, *perhaps they would have made a difference.*

But this was the war. What silver there was had gone, secreted away or taken along on a pilgrimage of death.

He jumped.

The wind hit him like an iron bar. He stumbled, lashed out at a wolf who was too close.

This was going to be *fun*. The bullets stopped as he landed, and now he had the square to himself. He felt the presence at his back quieten, shifting its attention to this creature who had fallen into its own private grievance.

Then, "*Vrolog!*" the voices screamed. *Vampire.* There was a hint of amusement in its combined voice.

The Rat turned, lashed out again, drew blood. His nails became long, sharp spikes. His teeth extended, fangs extruding. The world was painted red in front of his eyes; right here, right now, there was only one thing that mattered. Kill.

He looked for Mengale. Scenting the man, he followed a bloody path through the wolves, lashing, biting, hitting. The wolves, already weakened by the wind and the bullets, did not fight as hard as the first one, back in Brasov; by the time he reached the truck, where his senses told him Mengale was hiding, he had left the corpses of three young men behind him.

Seeing nothing but revenge in front of his eyes, the Rat broke the door to the truck as if it were a toy, and in one fluid motion threw himself inside.

The bullets struck him as he was airborne, slamming into him with hot, searing pain, throwing him to the floor. Through blooded eyes the Rat saw Mengale watching him levelly, carefully re-loading a revolver with gleaming bullets. Inside, the noise of the storm abated somewhat, and the Rat had a sudden feeling of unreal serenity, as if he were encased in a small, comforting cocoon, a metallic womb—or a coffin.

"It is fascinating," Mengale remarked, "The phenomenon of silver poisoning in vampires. I have had occasion to experiment on the more, shall we say, *unwelcome* members of the populace—communists, Jews, Gypsies—you know the type," he smiled casually at the Rat, "who happened to possess these particular *diseases*, but so few! I'm so glad I've found you." He aimlessly played with a couple of remaining bullets in his palm. "Teeth," he said. "Jewish teeth from my own foundry. Ironic, really, don't you think?" He levelled the revolver in the Rat's face. "It's been an extraordinary pleasure. It really has."

He pulled the trigger.

In the moment before the bullet erupted, the Rat

sensed a sudden calm. Ancient instincts took hold of his body, metamorphosing his physical shape. As his body began assuming, arduously, the rat shape, he rolled. In the moment the bullet fired, the source of the calm outside hit the truck with an unnatural force.

Sound came crashing back around them as the supersonic wave of the force tore through the truck and sent it flying in the air, propelling it upward and away. The Rat, half in human form still and half a rodent, slid helplessly down through the open doors, falling with a hard, painful impact to the ground. Above him he could see the truck, driven by the winds like a toy in the hand of capricious children, sailing over the market square and beyond the town's walls.

For a long moment the Rat followed the movement of the truck until, from far away, came the sound of a reverberating crash.

Then, at last, he passed out.

BUCHAREST, SEPTEMBER 1945

The Rat stood in the shadow of the great train station, looking dubiously at the newly purchased ticket in his hand.

It had taken a long time for his wounds to heal following the disastrous episode at Tirgoviste. Only months later, after his faithful partisans had operated on him yet again, pulling out silver bullets, preparing a shallow grave for the second time, scouring for blood, did he ask about Mengale.

There was no body found.

Tirgoviste's market square was nearly destroyed. The corpses of the *Wolfkommando* remained, and their bodies were carted to a common grave and set alight. The apparition of the old kings, of Tepes himself, had disappeared, and Castle Bran was once again inhabited by the living remnants of the royal family, the Queen and her children, cowering against the might of politics. Soon, they too would flee, and nothing would remain but a tourist attraction.

As the Rat languished in his makeshift grave, Romania turned. In August 1944, the Red Army marched into Bucharest, and by the beginning of 1945 Hitler was in his bunker in Berlin, surrounded on all sides by the allied forces.

It was the end.

And, the Rat had decided, it was also a beginning.

Draped in his new clothes, dark and unassuming, holding an English cigarette between his teeth, the Rat searched for the platform of the train to the coast.

The Old World was dying, its dark forces powerless in the face of what later philosophers would call the banality of evil. Humanity could provide more evil, more pain and suffering and humiliation, than any legend up in the Carpathians. It brought about a cold, efficient mass murder, and it had done so sitting civilly around the table, drinking tea and listening to orchestral music.

And the Old World was dying.

Decisive now, the Rat threw down the cigarette to the

floor, ground it with his foot and climbed onboard the train.

He was going to a new world. *The* New World.

The train, with a bellow of steam, pulled out of the station, heading for the coast and the shores of the Mediterranean Sea.

And in the small port in Greece, the Rat had decided, he would follow the rest of the war's survivors, the rest of the uprooted and the homeless.

In the words of so many before him, he would take ship to America.

The Rat settled down in the narrow chair, leaning against the window. He opened his coat pocket and took out the by now bruised and worn book, Stoker's book, and with the immigrant's hunger for the language of his new homeland, began re-reading the familiar passages as behind him the Carpathian Mountains disappeared slowly from view.

THE DOPE FIEND

This story has a special significance for me, being the first major "sale" I made as I was writing and submitting short stories. The initial inspiration was reading Marek Kohn's excellent *Dope Girls: The Birth of the British Drug Underground*, which tells the story of the principal characters—I merely twisted it to my own ends. I had no idea what to do with this story, which, at 15,000 words, was far too long to sell anywhere. Eventually, a friend convinced me to send it to Ellen Datlow at *Sci Fiction*—then the biggest and most prestigious online magazine—and, much to my surprise, Ellen published it. That was something for which I will always be grateful.

Mother's advice, and Father's fears,
Alike are voted—just a bore.
There's Negro music in our ears,
The world's one huge dancing floor.
We mean to tread the Primrose Path,
In spite of Mr. Joynson-Hicks.
We're People of the Aftermath
We're girls of 1926.

In greedy haste, on pleasure bent,
We have no time to think, or feel

What need is there for sentiment
Now we've invented Sex Appeal?
We've silken legs and scarlet lips,
We're young and hungry, wild and free,
Our waists are round about the hips
Our shirts are well above the knee

We've boyish busts and Eton crops,
We quiver to the saxophone.
Come, dance before the music stops,
And who can bear to be alone?
Come drink your gin, or sniff your 'snow',
Since Youth is brief, and Love has wings,
And time will tarnish, ere we know,
The brightness of the Bright Young Things.
– "Women of 1926" by James Laver

* * *

I'd known Edgar Manning for a number of years, and I
was there at the event that introduced him, rather noto-
riously, to the rest of London.

I was at Lizzie Fox's restaurant in Little Newport
Street. A group of us had been to the races the weekend
before, Mrs. Fox having had a weakness to the laying
of money on horses akin to mine. Lizzie won seventy
pounds. I'd lost a hundred, and another hundred on
champagne. Manning, who was also there, won, but not
as much as Lizzie.

Which is what started it all.

I'd been sitting in my usual place by the window, reading the paper, smoking. Watching the door. Watching Yankee Frank come in, his ugly face made even uglier by the cheap cigar in his mouth. He came straight up to Manning and demanded a pound.

"I have not a pound to give you," Manning said. His manners have always been impeccable, and his voice stayed quiet and calm.

"You're a fucking thief," Frank said. "I know how you're earning your living."

There was a moment of silence. London may have not, by that time, heard of Edgar Manning, but the people at Mrs. Fox's had, and that silence should have served as a warning to the faux-American.

Manning merely shook his head.

"You're a fucking shitpot," Frank said to him. I saw Manning's handsome black face go blank as he contemplated Yankee Frank's future. He may have let him go at that, but then Frank turned to Molly O'Brien, an actress and a slip of a girl who was sitting at a nearby table. "You're a bloody prostitute," he told her, chewing on his cigar.

Mollie may have been slight, but she wasn't one to take insults from anyone, and certainly not someone like Yankee Frank. "It's a pity you don't go and work for a living," she said to him. "You're only a ponce."

It was true—Frank's main form of income was from small-scale extortion of local hoodlums, an act commonly known as poncing—but it didn't mean he liked

Mollie calling him that. Before I could move he threw the cigar at her and punched her in the eye. Blood swelled up over delicate, white skin. "If there wasn't so many people in here, I'd do something else to you," he said, and ran out.

I looked at Manning; his face had closed even more, unreadable as a fetish mask, but it was open and kind when he asked Mollie if she was all right, before leaving a short while after.

What happened next became a legend, and it happened like this:

Outside, Mollie O'Brien ran into Yankee Frank again, who was walking with his brother, Charles. As I said, she didn't take crap from nobody, and she let him have it.

In turn, he punched her in the stomach and ran off. The two brothers then met up with a friend, Robert Davies, another lowlife.

They were just turning down Shaftesbury Avenue when, outside the Palace Theatre, they met Manning.

They attacked him.

Manning ran around a passing bus. Then he pulled out a piece, and, with careful aim, he kneecapped all three men.

* * *

This much is public knowledge. The *News of the World* delighted in the headline "Evil Negro Caught" and called Manning the "King of London's dope traffic." He was Jamaican, the son of slaves. A jazz musician who came to England from America during the war. He was always impeccably dressed, articulate, attractive.

In the event, he was sentenced to only eighteen months.

When he got out of jail he came to see me.

It was a cold November night; my apartment by the meat market of Smithfields was draughty. It was a bad night, and I did not wish to be disturbed. I had cleared the floor of all furniture and arranged half-melted candles in a Star of David on the floor, contained within a chalked pentagram.

I was about to begin when there was a knock on the door.

Outside, wet lights blinked in the dark. On the steps stood Manning, hat in hand: the time in prison had bulked him up, and his face looked lined and worried.

"Tzaddik, I need your help," he said.

"Come in," I said. He followed me into the hallway. "Sorry about the mess."

Manning took only a desultory look at the arrangements on the living room floor. He knew my working methods. I led him into the small kitchen and set to making tea while my guest sat down.

"I didn't know you got out," I said.

"It was only two days ago," he said. "And I've been trying to lay low for a while. Luckily my network of employees is still mostly in place. Here—" He reached into a coat pocket and took out a small paper packet, which he placed carefully on the table. "For you."

I didn't need to look in the bag to know what was inside. Nevertheless, I did. I placed some of the powder with care between my thumb and forefinger and snorted it, feeling exhilaration take hold of my brain.

"They don't call it joy dust for nothing," I said.

Manning nodded, but his face did not reflect my lightening mood. So, "What is it?" I said.

He looked up at me, his fingers wrapping around the mug of hot Earl Grey I had given him as if seeking to draw strength from it. "It's Billie," he said. "I've seen her. I don't know what to do."

I sat down opposite him and looked at his eyes carefully. His pupils were normal-sized, his eyes anxious.

"Billie's dead," I said.

Manning slammed a fist on the table; droplets of tea decorated the tabletop like liquid marbles. "I know that, Tzaddik!"

And then he started to cry.

* * *

Billie.

Billie Carleton.

The *World's Pictorial News* called her "The very essence of English girlhood." Billie Carleton, with her short cropped hair and large eyes that hinted at both tragedy and joy. A small, perfect mouth and a voice to match. I saw her in her first big performance, when she replaced Ethel Levey in the lead of *Watch Your Step* at the Empire. Charlie Cochran, who gave her that first break, later recalled her as "a young girl of flower-like beauty, delicate charm, and great intelligence."

She was also a cocaine addict.

I thought of those beautiful eyes, closed in death, and of a certain gold box I had kept, out of sight, in the sea-chest upstairs.

"She's dead," I said again.

Manning's voice, when it came, was dangerously quiet. "You and I both know, Tzaddik, that death is not an entirely unknown country."

"Isn't it?" I said. "I've never been there to know."

And Manning slowly smiled. White teeth made his mouth look like an ivory gate into the dark. "No," he said. "You haven't."

It is dangerous to deal with men who know your secrets. So, "Tell me about it," I said, and waited.

"I started seeing her two months ago," Manning said. "She came to me in prison. At first only in my dreams. Her face, as beautiful as I remembered it to be. She was trying to tell me something. Her mouth moved, but if she spoke I couldn't hear her."

"You were dreaming," I said. He ignored me.

"I got to a stage I didn't dare go to sleep anymore," he said. "She haunted me until I feared sleep." His tea stood untouched on the table. I pushed the bag of snow on the table toward him, and he helped himself to a pinch and snorted it. "So she began to appear when I was awake. Eighteen months, man, eighteen months of hard labour. I thought I was losing my mind."

"You still have to convince me you haven't."

He laughed. "She gave me this," he said, and reached into his pocket. "One night she came into the cell and touched me. I could feel her skin, warm and alive, and I could smell her, the scent of French perfume and lilacs. She gave me this," he repeated, and put a small, gold box on the table, watching me.

"A snuff box?" My voice was steady, my hands weren't. Manning could see that.

Well, damn him. I reached for the bag and helped myself to another pinch of cocaine. Damn Manning, I thought, and damn Billie too.

"Her coke box," he said. "The one that was resting on the table beside the bed the night she died." His eyes searched my face like a snake charmer watching his cobras. He noted the hands but didn't comment, and I gave him credit for that.

"Can you raise her?"

It was a request, not a question, and I had seen it coming.

"Possibly," I admitted. "Not a good idea. Not tonight. Not on any night." I was babbling, and in his eyes I could see he was reading me, not knowing but still guessing the source of my anxiety.

"Will you do it though?" Manning's large hands rested on the table, palms open as if in appeal.

"Can you not get a *houngan* to do it?" I said.

Manning laughed, short, dry laughter that sounded like a cough. "I tried. The *loa* are refusing to communicate with me. Apparently." His tone of voice suggested he was not much pleased with the *voudon* priest, and I suspected the man was probably dispatched himself as a sacrifice to Baron Samedi. Manning was not a man to tolerate incompetence.

I needed to think. I needed to buy *time* to think. "I'll have to make some enquiries," I said. "Also, some preparations. Where are you staying at the moment?"

He measured me up. "At the Montmarte Café," he said at last.

"With Zenovia?"

"Yes."

"All right," I said, decided. "I'll find you there. If you need to contact me, leave a message with Motty in the sandwich shop."

Manning smiled unexpectedly. "Motty still there?"

I nodded.

"Still dealing to the tourists?"

I smiled back. "We've all got to make a living," I said.

Manning nodded. The smile evaporated as he stood up.

At the door, he turned to face me. The expression on his face was unreadable. His hand felt warm and heavy in mine as we shook. He looked like he was about to say something, thought better of it. I watched him disappear into the darkness.

I shut the door against the outside and raced upstairs, searching for the box. But it was gone, and by then it was too late, and the darkness had already filtered inside.

* * *

At that time of the night—so late it was almost morning—Limehouse was shrouded in fog; a pack of small dogs rooted through the garbage outside the Shanghai restaurant, and from a distance came the muted sound of a late-night reveller stumbling out of an opium den and throwing up on the pavement.

There were no lights behind the windows of the Shanghai. I watched the place for a while, unseen, but no movement was visible. After fifteen minutes I gave up my watch and progressed down the causeway until I reached a small, unmarked door at the end of a narrow alleyway.

"You no come in." It took several loud knocks before the door was opened by a young Chinese man who stared at me with hostility.

"I'm looking for Chang," I said.

The lad looked blank. "No Chang here!" he said, and tried to close the door in my face.

"Not so fast, butterfly," I said, and pushed the door open again. I reached into my pocket, watching him. "My card."

He moved his hand away from the knife hidden in his coat and accepted it. When his head came up again, he was grinning. "So you're the Tzaddik? Sorry about that, you know what it's like around here at this time of the morning."

His sudden cockney accent could have broken glass, and there was something familiar about the shape of his face. "Are you related to Xing He?" I asked as he closed the door behind me.

His entire face lit up. "He's my uncle. Says you're the best player of pai-ke-p'iao he's ever seen."

"Don't believe everything he tells you," I said, and we both laughed. "Is Chang around?"

He shook his head. "You can wait for him here, if you like," he said. "I'll do you a pipe on the house."

He saw my face and lowered his voice. "From what I hear, he's got a new lady friend somewhere near Seven Dials. Should be back before too long."

Brilliant Chang always had a new lady friend. The son of a wealthy family based in Hong Kong, he drew women to him: I believe the *Sunday Express* once quoted a group of flappers who enthusiastically referred to him as "The rich young chink." I knew the man, and knew his methods: he once showed me the pile of identically-worded notes he carried everywhere in his pockets, to hand out like sweets to women who caught his fancy:

"Dear Unknown –" it said. "Please do not regard this as a liberty that I write to you, as I am really unable to resist the temptation after having seen you so many times. I should extremely like to know you better, and should be glad if you would do me the honour of meeting me one evening where we could have a little dinner and a quiet chat together. I do hope you will consent to this, as it will give me great pleasure, and in any case do not be cross with me for having written to you." It was signed, "Yours hopefully, Chang. PS—If you reply, please address it to me at the Shanghai Restaurant, Limehouse-causeway, E14."

"All right," I said to the young Chinese man. "I'll take you up on the offer." He smiled, and led me away into the main room of the house.

At this time of the morning few people were inside: two sailors in one corner, lying comatose with the glowing remains of a pipe still clutched in their hands; a man and a woman, with clothes that marked them out as members of the privileged class, sat together on large red cushions on the other side, similarly indisposed. Low-hanging lanterns cast dim light.

In yet another corner a man lay in shadows; the scent of incense wafted heavily throughout the room as did the pungent smell of burning opium. I took a seat on one of the cushions as my companion began preparing a pipe for me.

I let the sweet smoke fill my lungs and felt my eyes threaten to close as the drug took hold of me. As always, when it did, images of my expulsion from the Thirty-Six invaded my mind. *What are drugs to an immortal?* I shouted at them. They found me in the boarding house in Paris, in that other, even-dirtier century: I was lying comatose on the barren floor, my arms and legs bare and punctured, lying in my own excrement. The thirty-five other men and women of my circle, the hidden guardians of our people. Immortals, Guardians, Tzaddiks, call them what you will. In Hebrew the word means someone who is righteous: and they looked at me then with expressions ranging from pity to disgust.

Another breath of opium, and another, and the memory faded. The room receded into darkness, and I let my mind open, welcoming in a rare sensation of peace. There will be time, I thought, to tackle the problem of Billie Carleton. For now, let this be enough.

I watched the room with my eyes hooded. The toffs had finally got up and were escorted out of the room, a cab no doubt already waiting for them outside. The sailors, I decided, did not look like they were going anywhere in a hurry. My young Chinese friend was busy preparing another pipe for them.

And that person whose face I couldn't see... I watched the corner of the room and tried to guess at the features of the one who sat there. I felt a prickling at the back of my neck, as if I, in turn, was also being watched. I opened my senses wide, cast a net around the room. I felt the drug-induced haze of the two sailors, nightmares of raging seas and visions of monstrous creatures rising from the deep, felt the sweat forming on their skin, the taste of bloodied salt on their tongues. I tore myself from their shared nightmare and tried to focus on that corner of darkness I was after, but to no avail: it was as if nothing living were sitting there, nothing that could feel, or touch, or remember.

I rose from my seat and stepped toward the shadows, the pipe falling from my hand. But it was not my body that had stood: I was a pale, transparent form, a ghostly semblance of my body lying still and cold. I walked towards the darkness, my steps making no sound.

That corner of the room attracted and repelled me now. Its shadows thickened, became solid as walls. I thrust my hands into the darkness, drawing myself closer, intent on seeing the face hidden within.

My spectral hands formed shapes in the air, and a cold white fire burst from my fingers, penetrating the darkness.

There were not one, but two figures sitting there: two faces, clearly seen for the briefest of seconds, before a force I did not reckon on encountering hit my chest and pushed me violently back into my own body, where I lay, shivering and vomiting and no longer in the throws of delirium.

Two faces, glimpsed for the briefest of moments: I shivered again as I recalled Billie's beautiful diamond eyes looking into mine, and beside her, his hand on her thigh, a man with no face, whose body was shadow and bone.

* * *

I had my fingers wrapped around Brilliant Chang's neck and I wasn't about to let go. He hung against the wall, the expensive fur coat flapping in time to his legs kicking the empty air.

"What the *hell*," I said, "Did you get yourself involved in?"

I let him go and watched him fall to the ground, clutching at his neck and breathing hoarsely.

"I don't know what you're talking about!" he said.

"No?" I took the small gold box from my pocket and waved it in his face. "Do you recognise this?"

It was Billie's snow box. The box that had lain secure in my sea-chest since her death on that night at the Victory Ball in the Albert Hall. The box that, somehow, made its way into Manning's hand, given to him by a ghost.

Chang's eyes widened when he recognised it. "Where did you get this?" he said.

"Bill," I said, "Let me ask the questions, all right?" I was breathing hard, the after-effects of the opium dream hitting me in waves. "There was a man in your establishment earlier today. I want to know who he is."

Chang looked at me. We weren't friends, but we'd worked together in the past, and he could tell I was anxious and angry. I looked into his eyes and read understanding there, but also fear, a fear I was certain was not inspired by me. It was not an emotion I had seen in Brilliant Chang's face before.

I watched him think it through. Then, "Let me buy you a drink," he said, and rose up slowly to his feet. He looked at me and smiled lopsidedly. "You might need it. I know *I* do."

I had found Chang at Lily Rumble's flat off Holborn, alone and preparing to go out. I'd gone there straight from Limehouse: when I recuperated from the psychic attack, the mysterious man and his ghostly companion were gone, as if they had never been there. The young Chinese lad, Xing He's nephew, had also disappeared. A waiter at the Shanghai Restaurant finally gave me, after I coerced him, the address and swore Chang would be there. I left him to contemplate the prospects of the information proving incorrect and made my way to Holborn.

"All right," I said. I felt tired and angry and the thought of a drink was appealing. We left Lily's flat and walked the short distance to the Princess Louise. I followed Chang into the dim interior; Big Vi and Brixton Peggy were sitting in a corner. Dealing. When they saw Chang they began to rise, but with a look from him returned to their seats.

"Business good?" I said.

Chang shrugged. "You know how it is," he said. "Everyone wants the dust my girls sell."

I said, "Let's go upstairs."

The upstairs bar was even dimmer than below, and mostly empty. I scanned the room, but there was only the usual crowd in there, the lowlifes and the permanent drunks.

Chang ordered two glasses of cognac, and we took a seat in the corner by the windows. Chang pulled out two packets of twisted paper from his pocket, offered one to me.

"Ta."

The cocaine perked me up; the cognac soothed the edge of my anger. "Start talking," I said.

"It's to do with Manning," he said, and looked to see my reaction. He nodded. "I don't know what he's been up to in that prison: some fucked-up shit, by the sound of it. Way I hear it, he met some crazy *houngan* there. Someone not entirely human. Some awfully powerful horse being ridden by Samedi." He took a deep breath. "You know how he's been about Billie," he said, and it was my turn to nod. Manning had never gotten over her death, but I suspected Chang hadn't, either.

Chang looked reassured, but his face changed when he began to talk, his eyes narrowing. His fingers drummed a nervous staccato on the tabletop. "A man arrived at my establishment two nights ago," he said. "He was tall, almost gaunt, with a way of moving that reminded me of a cat. I can't recall his face clearly: all I could see were his eyes, emerald green and hypnotic. It was like a strange elongated skull mask with two pools of burning light where its eyes should have been." He shuddered and swallowed the rest of the cognac. "He knew every-thing! Every detail of every transaction; he reeled out the network to me as if it were a family tree. Every con-nection, every shipment, everything."

"What did he want?" I said. There was a strange feel-ing at the back of my head, a warning, like we were being watched. I scanned the bar crowd slowly, but it had not changed and I felt exposed, my nerves tingling in anticipation of attack.

"What did he want?" Chang gave a low, bitter laugh. "He wanted me. My organisation. To start with. I have seen things in my time, Tzaddik," he said, "But I have seen nothing like that man, if it was a man. He had power, and he held me helpless." He paused, and snorted more cocaine. His eyes were moving frantically in their sockets. "He told me you would come. He arranged to be there when you did. What did he want? Maybe he wanted you. I don't know. But I know this, Tzaddik: something Manning did brought this man here."

"How do you know?" I said. The sensation in the back of my head intensified.

Chang's fist hit the table. "Because I saw them! I followed him, you see, and I saw them! In Highgate cemetery, digging up the coffin of Billie Carleton!"

Something didn't ring true in Chang's narrative. "All right," I said. "Two questions. One, how do you know about Manning's *houngan?*" I didn't believe the story about the cemetery, but I wasn't going to interrogate him on that. There were more effective means at my disposal to ascertain the truth. They were never pleasant, but they were there and I knew I would have to use them.

"Two, if this man has the power you say he has, why did you follow him? And why are you talking to me now?"

Bill Chang smiled a slow, cold smile. "That's three questions, Tzaddik," he said. "*Technically.*" He signalled to the bartender, waited for two new glasses to arrive.

"Cigarette?" he opened a slim silver case and proffered it to me.

"No thanks."

He helped himself to a cigarette, lit it. Inhaled. The cold smile remained. "No-one fucks with me, Tzaddik," he said. "No-one. I don't care where that son of a bitch *moshushi* came from, he's not muscling in on my

territory. I fulfilled my part of the bargain. He wanted
to meet you. Knew you would come. If you ask me, it's
you who needs to start looking out."

He took a sip from his cognac and sighed. I knew
then that Chang was lying to me, that somewhere in the
last few days I had unwittingly walked into a maze of
danger and deceit, and had to step cautiously if I wanted
to survive it.

Chang tapped ash from his cigarette. A cloud of pale
blue smoke covered his face like a cloud heralding storm.
"As for Manning's witch doctor? Uncle Lee is in prison,
as you probably know. He told me the rumours. That's
all they are. All I know is what I saw. That Manning is
now free, and a grave-robber to boot, and that a *Feng-
Huang* is set loose in London. Make of it what you will."

While he was talking I was watching his hands.
Chang's hands were a lover's hands: Billie used to say
that. Long, sensitive fingers that trembled now, sending
smoke up in a crazy spiral. I watched his eyes, the quick
twitch in one corner; watched the sweat form on that
smooth pale skin. The feeling at the back of my head
refused to abate.

I knocked back the cognac and stood up. "Thanks for
the drinks," I said. "I'll be seeing you." He nodded at
me slowly.

I left him there and walked out, feeling like a rabbit
caught in the sight of an unseen gun.

* * *

I was caught in a web of lies, and somewhere—unseen but for a brief glimpse in Chang's opium den—somewhere was a spider, spinning the threads that threatened to bind me. I sat down in my armchair back at Smithfields and thought about the situation. On the one hand Manning, haunted by Billie's ghost, carrying with him the gold box that I had thought secure in my possession. On the other, Chang, with a strange story about a man with fiery green eyes and the power of suggestion.

I had seen for myself the power of the stranger, and found in it something that I recognised. Manning's people may have called it a *loa*; Chang's word for it was *Feng-Huang*. And in my own long history I had known ones who were like this mysterious entity, glimpsed from beneath darkened skies and on the edge of worlds beyond time...

My people called such beings *mal'achim:* angels.

I felt forced into doing something that was perhaps best left undone. There was danger here, and no clear motives, no understanding of the deeper powers at work. To have an angel materialise on the human sphere, on *Assiah*...I thought of my time serving with the Thirty-Six, and of a day and a night long ago in the deserts of Kush. Specifics evaded me like water flowing through grasping fingers. I had seen this before, but the memory was weak and unreliable, as is always the case with beings from the higher *Sephirot*.

It was time to make a decision, and so I did. My living room was already prepared: I redrew the symbols on the floor and lit the candles and placed protection about me, the symbols and icons of long-forgotten religions.

The candles flickered as I began the summons, and the wind howled outside, sending leaves fluttering against the windows like moths drawn to a flame.

A darkness formed in the heart of my chalked star, a cold and empty darkness as of space itself. Pinpricks of light appeared and disappeared inside it, and I could feel my power being tapped, drawn to feeding the portal between the spheres, between the *Sephirot*.

The lights in the darkness slowly grew, resolved themselves into a being of light. As if from a great distance the sound of beating wings was heard, rattling the glass of the windows.

"Tzaddik…" a voice whispered from the star. Eyes the size and brightness of suns regarded me. "You are still alive…How disappointing."

Not taking my eyes off it, this thing summoned from the sphere called *Binah*, Wisdom, I reached into my coat pocket and pulled out a small packet of snow. The bright eyes regarded me with hunger. I took a small pinch between thumb and forefinger and snorted it. Then I blew the rest, gently, into the circle of light, and the being inside it made it disappear.

"I want to know what it is that had made its appearance on *Assiah*," I said, when it had quieted.

A slow chuckle like the death of stars. "The Emanations are disturbed," it said. "The path from *Ketter* has been opened, and the Tree of Life itself is in turmoil. What have you done...human?"

The apparition's words disturbed me. "I have done nothing," I said.

The chuckle again, grating like a nail against glass. "Then perhaps that is the source of the disturbance," it said. "When the guardians do not guard, who will guard the guardians?"

"Wait!" I said. The burning figure was diminishing, the darkness of space returning to the place of summoning.

"*Quis custodiet ipsos custodes...*" whispered the voice, and the burning eyes closed, and were gone. The echoes of its mocking laughter resonated in the room, leaving me standing, alone and exhausted, in the thin light of candles.

* * *

"Manning's been looking for you, boss," Motty said. He stood behind the counter of the sandwich shop, chopping onions.

I slid onto a stool and opened the paper. Life was getting much too complicated, and I wanted a rest. I also needed the kind of information Motty and his boys could usually be relied on to supply.

"Thanks." I accepted the steaming mug of coffee and sipped the hot liquid.

"You want a pastrami and gherkin on rye with it?"

I smiled and lit a cigarette. "You know I do," I said.

"Sure thing, boss."

For the next ten minutes we didn't talk; I drank the coffee and settled down to enjoy Motty's creation. When I was done, I lit another cigarette and sat there, enjoying the momentary peace.

"Did Manning say what he wanted?"

Motty shook his head. "Said he needed to see you. Urgent like. Said you know where to find him."

I did. I just wasn't sure I wanted to.

As I sat in the rare sunshine, a half-smoked cigarette in my hand and a new mug of coffee on the counter beside me, I found myself going back to the night on the twenty-seventh of November and the Victory Ball, when lights were once again allowed to dispel London's after-hours darkness.

Billie wore a frock designed by one of her cohorts, Reggie De Vaulle: she looked stunning in it, like a butterfly awakened from a cocoon all ready to fly and dazzle. In the early evening she appeared in *Freedom of the Seas*. I was in the audience that night, and when the curtain fell I had felt a premonition, a fear. The curtain was about to permanently close on Billie Carleton.

The Victory Ball glittered with the ladies' jewels; the Brigade of Guards played *Rule Britannia*. Then came the dancing.

It was a night that lasted forever. The dancing didn't stop and neither did the trips to the lavatories, where men and women separately took cocaine to fuel their dancing. Billie had her gold box with her, and by the end of the night it was nearly empty. I danced with her once, and then she disappeared into the crowd.

It was a night that women ruled supreme. A night to welcome in a new era and lay to rest the old. Too many men had been lost on the battlefields of the Great War, and the change this had wrought was profound and, for many, unsettling. Billie danced all night, and the women of London danced all around her.

"Boss?" Motty's voice shook the memories away like drops of falling water. "I don't know what Manning was after, but there is something you should know."

I picked up the cigarette but it had run too low to smoke. I let it drop and helped myself to another. "What is it?"

Motty scratched his dark beard. He looked at me carefully. "Last night the boys were down by the Isle of Dogs. Helping remove a late night shipment, if you know what I mean." He smiled to himself. "They were nearly finished when they heard a dog barking at the river, loud enough to raise the dead." His smile vanished. "Or so they thought. You and I both know it takes more than a bark to..."

"Yes."

"They went over to check what the noise was about. When they came close enough, they saw it. It was a corpse."

I sipped the coffee. Corpses were not an unknown cargo on the Thames. They came floating up, bloated with gas, and lodged themselves in the reeds on the bank amidst the rest of the rubbish thrown into the river. For a corpse to remain unseen, it would need to be weighed down; letting it rise from the depths meant one of two things. Either the killer or killers were amateur, or they wanted the corpse to be found, as a message or a warning or both.

"Go on."

"It was a black man," Motty said. "His body was covered in faint blue tattoos from head to foot. Serpents and dragons and lizards; the boys said they seemed to move of their own accord, the lines glowing faintly in the moonlight." He sighed and rubbed his chin. "Boys."

I tapped the ash from my cigarette and waited. I had long ago found that Motty was not one to be hurried along. "Go on."

He lowered his voice. "It was a *sangoma*, Tzaddik. A *houngan*. Alfy Benjamin recognised him, even though the face of the corpse was frozen like a mask carved with fear. Alfy said he looked like he screamed for a long time; he said he looked as if, even in death, he was still screaming."

"You say Alfy recognised him?" I said. Possibilities were resolving themselves in my head, worrying me. "Where did he come across a *houngan*?"

Motty's answer was the one I was expecting. "In prison," he said. "Two, three years back. This guy was doing life with hard labour for some *muti* that went very wrong. Three people died, and a baby."

"I remember." There were rumours of a cover-up, that it was someone at Cabinet level who ordered the botched ritual. The *houngan*, as far as I could remember, remained quiet on that front. "What did the boys do?"

Motty shrugged. "What could they do? They cleared out as fast as they could. But I don't like it, Tzaddik. He was a powerful *sangoma*, that one was. Alfy, he said he saw him draw a window once on the wall of his cell. Said the window came alive, that there were things on the other side of that window he never wanted to see as long as he lived. Someone like that... Someone like that doesn't turn up floating in the river, Tzaddik. Not unless..." He left the thought unspoken.

Motty had given me a lot to think about. It seemed the story Chang fed me was at least partially true, and that meant I had to find Manning and get the truth out of him in turn. What worried me, though, was that the *houngan* was sent down the river as a warning: as a message, addressed to me. The *Feng-Huang* was after me. I just hoped he would stop skulking in the fog long enough for me to kill him.

"Thanks Motty," I said. "You and the boys try and keep out of this, all right? Keep out of trouble for a few days."

Motty winked at me across the counter. "We'll keep our noses clean," he said, mimicking putting snow to his nose and snorting it. "Don't you worry, Tzaddik."

I shook my head and walked out, into the dregs of the sunshine. Shadows were gathering over the old stone buildings and the alleyways, and I wondered if it would ever be possible to be rid of them. London was such a city, in which light and shade were inexorably bound. I feared the darkness that was circling around me, stalking me in the shape of the *Feng-Huang*. And I feared the thought of Billie, a ghost forced to return to the scene of her death. The dead should be left alone, should be left to death. To force them into a semblance, a mockery, of life, that was a crime, and for that violation I knew I would have to act.

* * *

The Montmarte Café was dark and smelled of vinegar and smoke. I came up to the counter and greeted Zenovia Iassonides, patron of the Soho Church Street establishment and Manning's unofficial business partner.

In the corner, two chorus girls were going over a script while blowing enough snow into their nostrils to kill an elephant. Cocainomaniacs, the papers called them, and they came to the café for Zenovia's true trade, not for her cooking.

She greeted me with a closed face. Zenovia was a hard woman to read.

"I'm looking for Manning," I said.

She snorted, and brushed a strand of greying hair from her temple. "Who isn't?"

I ignored that. "Is he here?"

Her hand took in the small, dank room and its shabby occupants. "Do you see him anywhere?"

I wasn't in the mood for games. "He wanted me to get in touch with him, and this is where he said he'd be."

I paused, then added, "Please don't answer that with a question."

She unexpectedly laughed. "It's good to see you, Tzaddik. Where have you been hiding?"

"In broad daylight," I said, and she smiled and nodded. "Best place to hide, Tzaddik. Best place to hide."

I thought of Manning's story, of Billie Carleton's ghost, and of the *Feng-Huang* walking the streets of London. It was not I who was hiding but Manning, and in his place, I thought, wouldn't I be hiding too?

"Come with me." She opened the latch on the counter and I came through. She took me to a small door underneath a wooden staircase that looked riddled with worms. She pushed the door open and pointed me in.

"Watch your step on the stairs," she said. "There isn't much light down there."

I thanked her and stepped through, and she closed the door behind me and left me in darkness.

The steps were stone, and old. I could feel a chill coming off them and taste moisture on my tongue. It was damp and humid and yet increasingly cold as I descended.

At the bottom of the stairs I stopped and let my eyes adjust to the scant lighting. There was a table there, covered in a grimy red cloth, with a single candle on it. There was a small cabinet, with nothing but a handgun on it, and a narrow bed.

"Edgar…" I said.

The body on the bed jerked up, a hand grabbing the gun from the cabinet and pointing it at me.

"It's me."

He looked at me with wild, unseeing eyes before some sort of sanity returned and he lowered the gun. "Won't do much good against you anyway," he said in an almost inaudible voice.

"No," I agreed. "And it won't do you much good against a *loa*, either."

His head snapped up. "What are you talking about?"

"Put the gun away," I said. He hesitated, then put it back on the cabinet.

"Good." I scanned the small subterranean room. "Do you have any opium down here? Or some alcohol?"

He grunted and reached for a drawer in the cabinet, pulling out a bottle of red wine and handing it to me.

I uncorked it and found two dirty mugs under the bed, which, after some thought, I poured the wine into.

"Drink this," I said. "I need you calm." I waited as he gulped down the red liquid. "You look like shit."

Some of Manning's old fire came back to him when he answered.

"Fuck you."

"Ah." I lit a cigarette and offered it to him, lighting another for myself. I hoped the smell of smoke would help mask the mouldy, decaying atmosphere of the cellar, but in the event I can't say the effort was overly successful.

"Now," I said. "Tell me the truth. Tell me about the *loa*."

I looked at him and waited. His face changed, anger

receding as a kind of dead man's hope crept into his eyes. Yet the overwhelming emotion on his face was fear.

"Tell me about the *loa*."

I did not want to use the word of my people, *mal'ach*. Angel. To do so would be to perpetuate a Christianised image of the word: of saintly, holy beings, granting peace and tranquillity and the touch of God. Those angels stared down at people from Church windows and from the pages of thousands of religious tracts, and I had no doubt it would have been a better, more just world if it were true.

"How much do you know?"

My patience was gone. It was not my job to play nursemaid to a man who had put me in danger, and it had been a long, long day besides. My fist hit his face and sent him reeling back, the cigarette dropping from his lips onto the floor. I grabbed him by the throat, lifting him up in the air and pinning him against the wall.

I watched as his feet tried to find purchase and failed.

"Don't fuck me about," I said. Each word was like a jagged knife I wanted to run across his neck. "You fucked up, Eddie. You fucked up big time. Now tell me what I need to know or you are going to find your skeleton in this cellar for the next hundred years with nothing but Billie Carleton's ghost for company. Do you understand?"

He was turning blue, but still he tried to nod.

"Good."

I opened my fingers, let him drop onto the bed, where he lay holding his throat and coughing. He tried to reach for the wine, but I knocked it out of his hand. The wine spilled like a pool of blood on the decaying mattress.

"Talk."

His words when they came were barely more than a whisper. "Prison was hard. They treated us like dogs. Worse, because the English value their dogs. They treated us like cattle, like we were nothing more than animals destined for the meat grinder. The wardens beat us, and at night the screams of the weaker prisoners could be heard echoing throughout the prison. We didn't treat each other any better."

He coughed and this time I poured him some wine. He drank it quickly and continued. "There was one prisoner nobody else dared treat this way. Not the wardens, not the prisoners. His name was Beauregard. Saturday Beauregard." Manning drew a shape in the air with his hands. "He was a big, mean badman. A *bull bucka*." He saw my expression. "Someone who butts heads with a bull, Tzaddik. A bully, and that's exactly what Saturday Beauregard was. That, and a *houngan*, a horse for Baron Samedi. I saw him when he was possessed, and you knew then that the only thing keeping him in prison was that he liked it. He *liked* it! He enjoyed ruling the prisoners and the wardens. He had a good life, like a king. And he liked breaking the weaker men most of all. The loudest screams always came from his cell." Manning shivered when he spoke, and his eyes looked haunted by memories. I offered him a cigarette, and he took it.

"Anyway, I got on with him all right. There were few enough black men in that prison, and Saturday was our boss. He had strange powers, but he was still a man. He liked talking, and he liked to hear stories, too. Also, he was a heroin addict. I think that was one reason he didn't escape. He needed a regular supply, and once he had the drug he didn't care much for anything. I still had my contacts, of course—I was only sent down for eighteen months—and so I ended up being his main supplier."

I listened. A strange feeling was forming again at the back of my head as if we were being watched. I got up and checked the stairs, but we were alone. I sat back down and let Manning continue.

"One night I slept badly. I dreamed, and in the dream I saw Billie, not dead but alive, walking toward me across a stormy sea. She seemed to walk on the waves, her hands reaching out to me, but when she finally came close enough to touch, her hands were as cold as marble and her hug was ice. I woke up then, and couldn't return to sleep. In the morning, Saturday picked up on it, and I was forced to tell him about the dream, and about Billie."

The feeling in the back of my head intensified. I stood up but again there was nothing. The cellar was silent save for Manning's voice.

"He knew who she was, and he enjoyed my discomfort. I think that's when he had his idea, though he only approached me several weeks later. When he found me he was shaking. He needed more heroin, and he had a proposition for me." There was something in Manning's face that made me think of an old clock, badly broken. I gave him another cigarette, and he continued.

"He said he could bring her back from the dead. That he had the power to negotiate with the Baron. In exchange, I would supply him with all the heroin I could get hold of, for free. I thought he was mad.

"You might not know what it's like when you're incarcerated, though I suspect that you do. For me, trapped in that prison, racked with dreams and held captive by a constant, dull fear, the thought was soon too much to bear. All I could think of was Billie, Billie's warmth against mine, Billie's laugh that was like a spring garden, Billie's humour, Billie's touch…

"After a week of that, I went back to Saturday, and I said yes."

I didn't hear any more. When the last word left his lips a cold, damp wind blew through the basement and the candles were extinguished. I heard the door at the top of the stairs move on its hinges as if caught in a storm, beating out a rhythm as it banged against the frame.

Without conscious thought I pushed Manning down, reached for his discarded gun, and in one move turned around and shot the figure standing at the bottom of the stairs.

* * *

He fell with a grunt of pain.

Human, then, and not the dark shape with the burning green eyes that I had half expected to be there.

More shapes moving on the stairs.

The gun rang out, once, twice, and two of them fell, but more kept coming in.

"Is there any way out of here?" I shouted to Manning.

One of the intruders reached the bottom and attacked. I felt a knife cut through my clothes and penetrate my skin. I twisted, broke the man's wrist, and plunged the knife into his eye.

More, jumping down from the staircase. There was a tattoo on the man's wrist, the one I had just killed.

A sword was thrust at my head. I ducked, kicked out at the attacker's face, and at his knees. He dropped with a scream, and I wrenched the sword out of his hand, using it to inflict wounds on two more of the attackers as they jumped down.

Then I was choking. Fingers were wrapped around my throat from behind, thumbs pressing into my windpipe. My elbow connected with the attacker's chest but didn't remove the pressure. I struggled, then found the pressure had lifted, and I could breathe again. Turning around, I saw my attacker on the floor, a bloodied gash in his head.

Above him stood Manning, and he was grinning.

"There's a way out through the sewers," he said. "If you could hold them for just a minute…"

He pulled the bed away from the wall. I turned back and into the whirling blade of another of the assassins. I broke his nose and watched him collapse. It was becoming difficult to move with all the bodies around, and more and more of the silent assassins were coming in through the door.

"Come on!"

Manning removed the bed; below it was a rug and a wooden box, which he opened. He pushed the rug with his foot, revealing a trapdoor. I ran towards him in a crouch.

"Get down there, I'll follow you," he said. There was a stick of dynamite in his one hand, a lighter in the other. He must have had them hidden in the box.

Edgar Manning, always prepared.

I jumped down the hole.

* * *

An explosion of heat above me and Manning dropped like a lead balloon, knocking into me. I fell into rancid water; a rat scuttled by, startled by the commotion.

It was a *big* rat.

"Who the fuck were those people?" Manning said as he got up. He looked dazed, but the grin on his face showed that, all of a sudden, he was enjoying himself.

I told him about the tattoo I'd seen. Manning let out a whistle. We were moving as fast we could through the sewers: the smell of excrement and waste was overpowering, and dirty water kept dripping on our heads and clothes from the metal ceiling of the pipe we were in. "Tongs? I didn't expect that."

"I did," I said. "I think someone wants you dead."

Manning turned his head: a man appeared behind us, and Manning shot him clean through the head.

"Or you," he said. "Which is the answer I find more likely."

I had thought of that, and the thought gave me no pleasure. Manning, on the other hand, seemed buoyant.

He led me through the glistening tunnels; there were no more followers. Our passage made the pipes reverberate and produce odd echoing sounds, and our feet splashed in the waste water.

"You don't want to be caught down here when they flood the sewers," Manning said, and moved his index finger along his neck with emphasis.

"I don't want to be caught down here at all," I said.

I followed him, but a feeling of foreboding began to steal over me. I was used to feeling the connection with the ground, with the skies, and now I felt that connection disappearing, barred to me behind the lead piping and the layers of earth. Down here elementals ruled, in a simpler and more dangerous world, a world closer to the Old World, a buffer zone between this world of *Assiah* and the outer *Sephirot*.

"Chang told me you dug up Billie Carleton's coffin."

He stopped and pushed me against the wall of the tunnel, his breath hot against mine. I didn't fight him. His face was hard, like iron that was smelt and remade in the furnace. "Then he lied."

"Did he?" I said. "It seems to me you both have an unhealthy interest in the dead."

He lifted his hand to hit me. I shook my head. After a moment he lowered his hand and continued walking.

"I could say the same for you," he said over his shoulder.

I trudged after him without an answer.

We were walking, it seemed to me, for too long. We had descended in Soho; surely there would be a manhole cover somewhere nearby? Instead, I felt our path was leading us further down, into the bowels of the city, and I was growing disturbed. I looked at Manning's back: he seemed to walk with a purpose in his step, leading me… leading me where?

"Stop," I said. The tunnels were getting darker and darker, and it was difficult to see. The air turned humid and hot, and deformed rodents ran in the murky water at our feet. "I said stop."

He didn't seem to hear me.

"Manning!"

I watched him disappear into the shadows ahead.

I looked at my surroundings, sighed, and moved on to follow him. From a coat pocket I removed a small packet of snow and snorted it. I thought of Manning: he'd seemed scared when he came to see me, and scared again in the basement, and yet the fighting seemed to have revived him. And now he was leading me through the sewers like a *Dybbuk*, a man possessed. I thought of simply knocking him out, but then where would I go? I didn't want to leave him down here, and I had no idea how to get out. I was, literally, out of my depth.

Somehow, the thought made me giggle. I felt happier now, as if decisions and their making were no longer important. I followed behind Manning as we walked further and further into the bowels of the earth.

* * *

We walked in silence, the only noise produced by the treading of our feet in water.

I followed Manning through turnings in the sewer system, into tunnels that were made of stone; clumps of moss grouped together for comfort on the cold walls providing a faint luminosity. There were writings on the walls, letters and drawings that I felt I should recognise and yet didn't.

The quality of light changed: as we journeyed I began to notice strange crystal globes set in the walls, emitting a clear, bright light.

After more time had passed, the tunnel we were in began to widen and at last came to an end in a cavern of white stone. Here the light was brilliant and yet comfortable. Crystal globes were set at regular intervals along the walls, turning the cavern into the semblance of a ballroom, or a temple.

On the floor of the cavern was a giant drawing, and when I saw it my mind returned to me. It was the Tree of Life.

A dark snake was coiled around the Sephirot. Its tail was touching *Malchut* and its head was by *Keter*.

Beside me, Manning's face slackened, then closed.

Without a sound the big man fell to his knees and then to the floor, where he lay with a look of peace on his face.

As he'd fallen, the lights had dimmed. I kneeled down and took his pulse. Manning's heart was beating a strong, steady beat. He looked like a man in the throes of a deep, drugged sleep.

Nothing stirred amidst the newly formed shadows. I opened my mind and let it encompass the cavern. Slowly it expanded, and yet I encountered the presence of no living being, only a kind of ancient, drowsy solitude that seemed to emanate from the stones themselves.

"Tzaddik."

I turned, my mind shrinking back to one focal point from which I tried to see the speaker. The voice was feminine, and somewhat familiar, like the taste of vintage Judean wine sampled a long time ago and never entirely forgotten.

She stood in the drawing of the Tree, in the heart of the Pillar of Equilibrium, over the sphere called *Tiph'eret*, Beauty. Her hair was short, where I remembered long; white, where I remembered the blackness of strong coffee.

"Amat..."

She laughed. I remembered her laughter, but it was buried deep, under the layers of memories that recorded every detail of her death, the screams as she fought the Leviathan in the old Egyptian kingdom and was pinned by the dying god into the mud of the Nile, her body broken and the magic whispering as it ebbed away... Amat al-Qadir, Servant of the Almighty.

Under her feet the dark snake came alive. It crawled from the Tree of Life and wrapped itself around her like a scarf. Reptilian eyes regarded me; a forked tongue hissed as it tasted the air.

"It hardly seems credible that you are alive," I said.

She nodded. A small smile caught at the corners of her mouth like a butterfly threatening to escape. "Hardly," she said, and we both laughed.

"Come here, fallen guardian," she said. I walked to her. She held her hands to me, but when I touched her I felt nothing, only whispering air. I looked into her face, no longer smiling. "You died."

She inclined her head in agreement.

"The paths between the spheres are disturbed," Amat said. "The passage of those seeking an end to death has unbalanced the twenty-two ways."

I stood back and looked at her, feeling both sad and annoyed. "Don't you think I know that?"

She shook her head. "It isn't a question of what you know, it is a question of what you *do*."

"Amat," I said. "You can drop the sphinx act. I'm too old for riddles, and I am no longer bound by the code of the Thirty-Six."

She smiled at that, and it brought back memories of her and Ma'ani and Sarwa—the three golden girls of the hidden temple—in days long gone, when the sun seemed never to set and the waning and waxing of the moon were reflected in the Nile and in the lives of our people. Still, I felt the old bitterness rise in me again.

"You were always a rake," she said gently, and I felt the anger pass as swiftly as it had materialised.

"I've come to deliver a message," she said. Her hands stroked the snake, and its tongue hissed against her skin, scenting her. "There is a thing let free on *Assiah* which is not meant to be so." She looked into my eyes and said, "And it is your problem."

"Strictly speaking," I said, "It's the Thirty-Six's problem."

Her eyes betrayed amusement. "Oh, they will probably move in if you can't solve it," she said. "But of course, you'd be dead by then."

"And wouldn't that be just dandy," I said. But I thought about her words, realised they had hidden a warning. There was something on *Assiah* that could kill a Tzaddik. No wonder the Thirty-Six were sitting it out, hoping I could do the job for them or, even better, finally die in the process. I thought about my old comrades and decided I'd rather stick around, if only to give them a two-fingered salute.

"Is that it?" I said, feigning a confidence I didn't quite feel.

That smile again, returning with its parasitic host of unwanted memories.

"That's it," she said. "No more 'sphinx act', all right? You know the consequences of failure or success."

"Fine," I said. I had always found it difficult to argue with Amat. I reached out with my hand, wanting to touch her one last time, to feel her hair between my fingers, to say good-bye. But again there was nothing there, like a mirage painted on air.

I looked around me, at the cavern and the painting on the floor. "What *is* this place?" I said.

"A hiding place," Amat said. "During the riots and blood libels of Richard the First's rule, a group of rabbis—with an understanding some say has never been surpassed since—built this place as a refuge for our people, deep under the king's city."

"It couldn't have done them much good," I said, thinking of the expulsion of the Jews from England in 1290. I had never heard of a secret dwelling underneath London, or of the mysterious rabbis Amat talked about.

"Their understanding of the *Zohar* was unparalleled," Amat continued. "They utilised…"

I let her speak as I opened my mind again to my surroundings. In life, Amat loved to show off her knowledge, and it seemed she had retained the tendency in death. Still, I could not detect her presence. My mind moved over the curious crystals and their cold light, sensing nothing. Beyond one of the walls I felt space, and within it giant, hushed figures. My mind moved over them, sensing enormous bodies made of clay: statues, perhaps? My mind moved around them, then shrank back as I detected a slow, regular beat coming from them. Were they alive?

I looked at them in my mind's eye. They *were* enormous, each easily the size of ten men, and the clay they were made of seemed ancient. Their faces had no features, and their hands were closed into fists. Hard diamonds were strewn in a pattern throughout their body, a pattern I had just recognised.

They were imbued with the Tree of Life.

"Enough," Amat said. I returned to myself and stood facing her. On the floor beside me, Manning snored loudly. "Time is running out, and the angel is growing stronger. It will come looking for you. Be prepared."

"I thought you were going to quit the Sibyl role," I said, but her eyes mesmerised me. I was lost in them, seeing the faraway shapes of curious mountains and rivers, clouds that seemed like faces, and giant creatures gliding on the winds… I reached for her, a third and futile time, and felt pain explode in my hand like a grenade.

"Remember me…" she whispered, as the snake's venom coursed through my blood. I felt a hot, searing pain as if my brain were exploding.

Then I passed out.

* * *

I came to on the floor of my living room. My hand throbbed. Two puncture marks were visible on the flesh between my thumb and forefinger. I stood up. Underneath my feet was my chalked Star of David. Around me, furniture and belongings lay in broken heaps.

I moved through the house, feeling weary: room after room had been smashed up and its contents scattered. There were pools of piss in the bedroom and human excrement left on the kitchen's floor.

I didn't care about any of that. I went down to the basement, not surprised to find it had also been ransacked. The false brick in the southern wall, however, was undisturbed. I slid it out and helped myself to its mysteries: a bottle of Scottish whisky, a small bag of opium, and a curved wooden pipe, the shape of a wingless bird. There were also some vials I had left there for a day of need, and these I pocketed carefully.

Then I proceeded to have a party.

It went well as far as solitary parties go, and when there was no more whisky and only a little cocaine I curled up into a ball on the floor and went to sleep, figuring a house that had already been broken into might just be the best place to lie low for a little while.

I slept, and in my sleep Amat's face returned to haunt me, uttering more nonsensical warnings; I saw the dark figure of the *Feng-Huang* stalking shadows, moving through my dreams, but he never turned back, never turned to look at me. I followed him through dreamscapes of torn memories, returning at last to the boarding-house in Paris, to a self centuries in the past, lying on the floor, choking on vomit, body wracked by drugs.

It occurred to me, then, that my life had not, perhaps, changed as much as I thought it had.

In my dream, the *Feng-Huang* loomed over me and laughed. Its eyes were burning emeralds, poisonous green, and its laughter was that of the hyena, a mad, deep sound that hurt my skull.

I tried to turn away from it, and in the way of dreams

the scene was somehow gone, and I was dancing in the Albert Hall, Billie Carleton in my arms, the band playing music that made us soar together like two birds tied by a string. I could see Manning sitting at a table by the bar, Brilliant Chang opposite him. They were playing cards, their faces grim, and the pot was Billie's golden snuff box.

Their cards, I noticed, were Tarot cards, and I strained my neck to see who would win the game, but the swirl of dancing partners passed between us and when I looked again they were gone.

"You smell lovely tonight," I said to Billie, and she smiled at me and held me tight, and so we danced until the ballroom was gone and only the two of us remained, dancing in a perfect darkness, our lips touching in one blossoming, perfect kiss.

As I tasted her I felt her move away, become lighter. "Billie, no!" I cried, but her form began to melt in my hands, to ebb away, and I cried and tried to hold her, to keep her, all to myself.

Then somebody kicked me hard in the ribs and I woke up shivering on the basement floor.

* * *

"You son of a bitch," I said. Motty put out his hand and helped me to my feet.

"Sorry, boss," he said. "We tried waking you up but you were gone. And time is something we don't have an abundance of right now."

He motioned for the boys, who were leaning against

the walls of the basement. Aviel brought forward a flask of hot tea and a bag full of sandwiches, then retreated and lit himself a cigarette.

"Thanks."

The hot tea washed away memories and dreams alike; I ate quickly, while Motty and the boys waited. Then, "What's going on?"

"We've been trying to find you since yesterday," Motty said. "Zenovia came to the shop screaming murder. Said that you and Manning had been attacked by tongs, then disappeared. We came to your house, but it was already broken into. I left Daniel outside to watch if you came back, but being the useless boy that he is it took him until now to let me know."

The boy foremost left shook his head. "It wasn't my fault, boss. This whole area is crawling with police."

"Why police?" I said. I had a feeling I would not like the answer.

Motty coughed. It wasn't a gentle cough, but the cough of a smoker who had pursued tobacco with a passion. "You're wanted for the murder of Saturday Beauregard."

I opened my mouth. Then I closed it. Then I said, "Fuck."

The boys all nodded.

"According to the papers," Motty said, ploughing on as if determined to unburden himself of the bad news as quickly as he could, "Beauregard escaped prison the night after Manning was released. And according to eyewitnesses, he was seen in Limehouse, and later again he was seen having a fight with a man matching your description. Also–" the cough stopped him again, but only briefly "–his body was found last night, downriver from the place we saw him. You're wanted for questioning."

"Very convenient," I said. I thought about the situation. The Metropolitan Police were not known for moving very fast, so their quick mobilisation must have had an external agent of some sort. It didn't take long to work out who—or what—was behind it.

"Any word of Manning?"

"No," Motty said, a faint note of surprise in his voice. "We thought he was with you."

"Clearly," I said, "He isn't."

There was a noise from upstairs, and Alfy Benjamin came rushing down the stairs.

"Looks like we were spotted," he announced. "There're pigs and tongs all over this area and they seem to be heading this way. Separately, of course, but this looks like trouble."

I motioned the boys, and they followed me as I climbed back up to street level. The time for running around and being pursued was over, or so I tried to tell myself.

Through the window a dull afternoon light cast a tired haze over Smithfields market. I had lost twenty-four hours according to Motty, though I suspected my time in the sewers and my time in the dream were somehow longer than that. There were plainclothes policemen milling about in the street, trying unsuccessfully not to look like policemen. There was also a large contingent of Chinese men, sticking to the shadows in the entryways of buildings. It almost made me want to find a way back to the sewers. But not quite.

"Where one sees only a problem," I said, "another sees opportunity."

"What are you going to do?" Motty asked.

I turned to him and grinned. "I'm going to magic us away," I said.

"Oh. Good," he said. He didn't look reassured.

We left through the front door. Me in the middle, surrounded closely by the boys. Alfy and Motty strode ahead, shouting for the crowd to make way, that a dangerous criminal was caught. The policemen were close, and were approaching us now, but we continued to move, directly toward the tongs.

It was a dangerous game to play, with me as bait and the boys with the very real chance of getting hurt. But it was a game worth playing.

I could almost see it in their eyes, the moment the decision was made. The tongs wanted me. And they hated cops. On the other hand, the cops wanted me. And they really hated the tongs.

I heard the shot go off as planned. Motty, soon followed by another, this one from a policeman. The tongs returned fire.

I watched the riot begin.

"Since when do the police have firearms?" I shouted

and felt exhilaration grip me like a vice. "Watch out, boys—it's magic time!"

I took out the two large vials from my pocket and broke them with a flourish against the ground. Rancid smoke enveloped us.

I hit out, as a man—I couldn't tell which faction he belonged to—charged at me, and then we ran, me and the boys, while behind us smoke billowed and guns sounded and the whole of the street descended into a manic, wild brawl.

* * *

A guy came through the door with a gun.

He put the gun into his belt as he came in and took off his hat. The face—leathery and tough and wrinkled and as pockmarked as the face of the moon—curved into a smile.

"Shalom, boys," he said cheerfully. His voice was American, soft, well-articulated. I could see Alfy and Motty tense beside me.

"Adam," I said. "How are you?"

He laughed. "It's good to see you too, Tzaddik. I hear you've landed yourself in trouble again."

I made a sign, and the boys got up and filed out of the door. When we were alone, I motioned for him to sit down and poured him a glass of brandy from the crystal decanter. We were in a safe house in Hampstead. At least, I hoped it was safe. In any case, I did not intend to stay long.

Adam Worth regarded me with a smile. He brought out a small silver case, opened it, offered me a cigar. When I declined he took one out, returned the case into the hidden pocket in his coat, and took great care in trimming and lighting it. Fumes rose in the room like an ill wind.

I watched him in silence and waited for him to speak. Adam Worth, the man Sir Robert Anderson, the head of Scotland Yard, once called "the Napoleon of crime"; the man who inspired Doyle to create his fictional Moriarty.

"I thought you were dead," I said.

"Did you?" he shrugged. "I am under *that* name. The Civil War—though why for God's sake they call it that I have no idea—ended some time ago. It was time to assume a new *rôle*."

"What do you want?" I didn't need this complication. And I didn't want anything to do with Worth, regardless of what he was calling himself in these more enlightened times.

"Do you know," he said, puffing on the cigar and looking at me keenly, like an interested father, "Pinkerton once said that 'in the death of Adam Worth there probably departed the most inventive and daring criminal in modern times'? He said that of all the men he had known in his lifetime, I was 'the most remarkable criminal of them all.'" He smiled and shook his head as if remembering better times and better days.

"Did he?" I said. Then I had to smile. "You were always a great thief."

Worth waved his hand in false modesty. "You're not so bad yourself, when you put your mind to it."

"So what do you want?" I said again. He shook his head at me, admonishing. "You fucked up, boy," he said. "There's a ghost and an angel on the loose in your city, and you seem to think hiding here and drinking brandy is the answer to all your problems. Look how long it took me to find you. If you're trying to hide, you're not doing a very good job of it."

"I'm not trying to hide," I said, annoyed. "I'm trying to think. I don't understand what's going on."

"Don't you?" We were indulging in the Jewish Dialogue: trading a question for a question for a question. He dropped his ash carefully into the ashtray. "Or is it because, for you, the ghost is more than a ghost and you are reluctant to face her? No, don't answer that," he said. "I understand no-one knows exactly what happened on the night Billie Carleton died, and I'm sure that's only right. I also know a small gold-plated snuffbox that she habitually carried on her person could not be found when the police got to her room, though I've heard it's been seen recently around town."

I watched him, this fat, immortal Jew, who sat like a contented spider in his web of information. I should have been flattered he was here at all, but I remembered Genoa, and the murder there. I was not the only one to be expelled from the Thirty-Six over the long, long years.

"The heart of the mystery," Worth said, "Is at the heart. *Cherchez la femme*, ah?" He winked at me and blew a smoke ring that turned into Billie Carleton's face before ebbing away.

"Impressive trick," I said, but I was rattled. Worth had come here to tell me something. Time was running out, and I had to act.

"What do you mean?"

He stood up, drew out his gun, twirled it on his finger; raised it to his lips and blew smoke from the barrel. "I'll be seeing you," he said. "Or not. As the case may be."

He walked out of the room, putting the gun into his belt as he did so, leaving me alone to think of a woman, and her grave.

* * *

Cherchez la femme, Worth said, and so I had come at last to find her: the night was moonless and the skies patterned in stars, and the tombstones projected, ghostly and grotesque, over the lengthening fog that lay like a thick residue on Highgate Cemetery.

I had taken some coke beside the gate to the cemetery, afraid of what I might find inside. Dubious of Chang's story of the desecrated grave and yet apprehensive. I felt my consciousness grow as the drugs took hold of me and knew the ways between the *Sephirot* were wide open tonight. The *Feng-Huang* might not be the only thing to walk *Assiah* on this night.

Her grave lay undisturbed and modest beside two larger graves, one sporting an angel with wings unfurling, the other a curious figure: an innocent, androgynous child with eyes of stone that caught the distant light of stars. As I approached it, the feeling of dread at the back of my head intensified.

I turned—and found him. A piece of darkness detached from the night.

The *Feng-Huang* laughed.

It was a deceptive sound, full of the warmth of a spring day and the lucidity of lake water, and yet it made my skin go cold as if a skeletal hand had laid bony fingers on my wrist.

We stood facing each other without movement, without sound. He was tall and dressed in a black, flowing robe that formed a closed circle on the ground. His face was hidden in shadows: only the green eyes burned within the darkness.

The eyes found me and held. Finally, he spoke.

"You are like a ferret, set on a scent and left to run and run in circles until you reach its source," he said. "You are no longer dangerous, but you may be useful."

"Fuck you," I said.

The *Feng-Huang* laughed again. "I don't think so," he said. The fire in his eyes intensified.

Burning pain burst in the back of my head, and I fell to the ground.

Hands grabbed me. Hauled me to my feet. I felt my hands being tied behind my back.

"Your rivals for the affections of the delightful Ms Carleton," the *Feng-Huang* said. As he did, two figures materialised in front of me.

"Hello, Tzaddik," Chang said. "You took your time getting here." He was dressed in flowing, vaguely oriental robes, his dark hair tied back in a ponytail. In his hand he held what seemed to be a very sharp knife.

But the man I was watching was standing next to Chang. Edgar Manning wore a calm expression, but the pupils in his eyes were abnormally large. In his hand, too, was a knife. I was getting a bad feeling.

"To bring the dead back to life," the *Feng-Huang* said, "Can only be done at a perilous exchange. A normal human life would not do, as that exchange is only equal. You understand?"

Chang and Manning nodded, the motion mechanical like that of automatons.

"To give the dead life," said the *Feng-Huang*, "an immortal life must be sacrificed."

"You didn't think I came here alone, did you?" I said, trying for a bravado I didn't quite feel.

"That is exactly what I think," said the *Feng-Huang*. "Like I said, you were like a ferret, led on a leash. You believed Manning when he lied to you. You believed Chang when he, in turn, fed you the rest. And you believed them because each was telling you some of the truth, and you were too weakened by your drug habit to comprehend the whole."

"I've had a perfectly healthy drug habit for many years," I said. The *Feng-Huang* laughed. "Manning was the fool who asked Saturday Beauregard for help in raising Billie's spirit. And Beauregard was a fool for consenting, and for trying to take on powers far beyond his control. But we are all pawns in somebody else's game, Tzaddik. Even you and I. For Manning, there was another man who moved the pieces on the board."

"Chang."

The *Feng-Huang* moved the darkness that was his hooded head in assent. "Chang wished to have his mistress back. And so he used one of his men, a man by the name of Uncle Lee, to impress upon Manning the idea of the summoning. But he was useful, too: for all his bravado he is mine, now."

"And so," I said, "all the actions of mortal men led only to bring forth a creature like you onto this earth. Compelling stuff, I'm sure, but I do not play games with either mortals or angels. *You will not be allowed to remain.*"

As I spoke my fingers moved, analysing the knot. The *Feng-Huang* had wanted me out of his way, wanted me chasing reflections in the fog as he waited for this night, the night when the spheres were aligned and the spirits of the dead—as well as those of the living—could travel across the *Sephirot* with relative ease. He set me on a goose chase, planting the seeds that would lead me here at last, to this lonely grave in this place of the dead.

"She meant a lot to you, didn't she?" he said. "Would you like to see her again?"

I didn't answer.

"No? A pity."

The *Feng-Huang*'s eyes rose in flame. He extended his

arms as if in an embrace—and into the darkness of the night materialised the face of the woman I once loved, and lost.

"Billie…" The word was drawn from our collective throats. Chang and Manning and I, together, under her power still.

Her face was white and beautiful, as always. But her eyes were dark and vacant, the eyes of the dead, and when I looked into them I saw only the abyss between worlds.

"Release her!" I said.

My tormentor laughed again. "At what price, Tzaddik? Would you sacrifice your life so she could live again? Or would you have me send her back to death?"

"She is already dead," I said. "and what you have there is only a pale and empty copy of the woman that was Billie Carleton. You could never bring her back—such a thing is beyond your power and mine. Listen to me, Chang!" I said. "And you, Manning. She is dead, gone, and you must let her be!"

Chang slowly shook his head. "I don't think so," he said. "Why is it that I, the son of an ancient and powerful culture, am here in this city, in this place and time, treated like an animal? A menace? They call me a Dope Fiend, the Yellow Plague, when I am a man with a heart as good as any Englishman's. But they would never let me and Billie be. And you could say the same for Manning, Tzaddik. Or indeed for you."

"You don't understand," I said. "She is dead. Truly

dead. This creature is preying on your desires for his own ends."

"Then so be it," Chang said with sudden anger. "I have made deals with worse and survived."

"Unlikely," I muttered.

And then, like in a nightmare one expects but dreads all the same, Billie spoke.

Her voice was flat, lacking the exuberance, the joy and excitement of her living days. It was the voice of a ghost, but a familiar one, and I knew what she would say before she said it.

"My box," she whispered, her dead eyes finding mine. "My golden snuffbox. Why did you take it?"

The *Feng-Huang* turned his eyes on me; there was malicious glee in their burning essence.

"What is she talking about?" Manning asked. "Billie, what do you mean?"

"She means," the *Feng-Huang* said, "that the Tzaddik is the one who removed her little box of poisons from her deathbed. Perhaps you'd care to ask him why?"

"Why, Tzaddik?" Manning said. There was real anguish in his voice, and I realised then, with a springing of hope, that he and Chang were not yet entirely under the *Feng-Huang*'s control, that he was waiting to see if he could use them without destroying their minds. And it gave me a chance.

"He gave me the pills," the thing that was once Billie Carleton said. "The pills I took, after the ball. They made me fast and happy and filled me with energy."

"What did you give her, you bastard?" Chang said, and I was aware of the knife in his hands moving towards my face.

I sighed. My fingers worried at the knot, loosening it. I had to hope talking would keep me away from the *Feng-Huang*'s ultimate purpose, at least temporarily.

"I gave her the pills she asked for," I said, suddenly weary. "I gave her everything she asked for."

"She didn't die of the cocaine, did she," Manning said, and his knife, too, was rising towards me. "She died of the pills you gave her."

"I died," Billie said. Her empty eyes looked into mine. "I died for you."

"You never loved me," I said. "You never loved any of us."

The *Feng-Huang* moved. It was like mercury, heated up and sliding on pure glass, the movement inhuman and frightening. "Enough," he said. "Gentlemen, I have offered you a deal. For your love to live, an immortal must be sacrificed. Please don't let me keep you from your job."

"Stop!" I said. The knot was nearly untied. Chang and Manning looked at me. Their eyes were still their own. I had hope. "Believe me. If there was a way to bring her back, I would gladly do whatever is needed to do so. But the dead must remain so. It is the law of nature. To undo it would be to destroy everything."

"He is lying!" the *Feng-Huang* said. "Kill him, mortals, and you will have your woman."

Would they do it? How much were they blaming me for? They raised their knives.

"Chang! Manning! Please!"

And then my hands were free. I raised them as the *Feng-Huang* howled, and I drew a symbol in the air. Chang and Manning blinked, looked around. When they saw Billie they both looked scared.

"Is that what you want?" I said. "A ghost? That is all she will ever be."

"No," Chang said. And again, "No!" And he moved the knife in an arc and sliced at the *Feng-Huang*'s throat.

"Chang!"

The *Feng-Huang* roared; he took hold of Chang and threw him in the air. Chang's head hit a tombstone with a sickening sound, and he lay still.

"Go, Edgar!" I said. "Go!"

Manning moved slowly away, the knife held in front of him.

"This is between you and me, angel," I said. "The road between the spheres is open tonight, and I suggest you take it back to where you came from."

"You," the *Feng-Huang* said, "are going to die."

"I don't think so," I said. While standing in the cemetery with my hands tied, my foot had been able to draw, again and again, a symbol in the ground. Now, I moved away from it.

On the ground where I had stood was a Star of David, etched deeply into the soil as if branded there. "Clay and magic," I said. "and the Tree of Life." There was a small leaf, half broken, embedded in the circle. I hoped it would work.

"What is this?" the *Feng-Huang* said. "This is nothing. Is that the best you can do?"

He didn't wait for my answer. The clothes containing him drew and tore, and out of them grew the true darkness of the angel. It was a darkness such as encountered in an underground river that had never seen the sun, the darkness of the inside of snails, of the other side of the moon, of death. It grew, threatening to absorb me, to touch Chang's unmoving body, to engulf Manning as he stood there, uncertain, the knife in one hand.

The earth shook.

It shook with the fury of an earthquake. The darkness that was the angel hovered above, suddenly unsure.

And from below the graves they rose: the beings I had glimpsed beneath the foundations of London, the buried, secretive giants.

They were creatures of clay, and yet the lifeblood of the Tree surged in them, the strongest I had ever seen or felt. They had arms like tree trunks, and as they rose out of the earth they took hold of the angel, the *loa*, the *Feng-Huang*, and held it.

It screamed.

It screamed for a long time as the great golems descended back into the earth; screams that could still be heard, echoing in my ears, from far below the ground.

"Tzaddik." It was Billie, and the voice was her own, that voice I had fallen in love with, the voice that

commanded me and entreated me, and got me to supply her with the drugs that were to kill her.

I turned, and her eyes were once again her own, lov-
ing and happy and mischievous.

"I am sorry, Billie," I said. "I am so, so sorry."

"I know," she said, and she moved towards me, growing insubstantial as she did. "I know."

And then she kissed me. Her lips touched mine, for
the longest second I can recall. And then she disappeared.

* * *

"Was it a dream?" Manning said.

We were sitting in the upstairs bar of the Princess
Louise. There were only the three of us: the Jamaican,
the Chinese, the Jew.

"No," I said. "Though I wish it was."

Chang returned to the table, carrying with him a tray
with three more glasses of bourbon on it.

"Future generations will judge us," he said, and cut
three lines of snow on the table. We each snorted one.
"And perhaps, after all, they will not judge us, nor Billie,
too harshly."

"I'll drink to that," I said.

UGANDA

I have long been fascinated by the story of the Zionist expedition to British East Africa in 1904, one of the strange and little known chapters of history that can provide such a pivotal "what if" moment for writers. I managed to hunt down the report on microfilm, and the entries reproduced herein are indeed real, though I took my own sideways slant to the expedition's unlikely journey...

The following is a collection of documents found in the archives of the Wiener Library, London. What follows next are copies of two diary entries in what appears to be Theodore Herzl's handwriting. In the first, the paper is brittle and badly smudged, almost as if it had been in a fire. The edges are roughly torn. It is dated five months before Herzl's death. The second is the most well-known of his diary entries.

* * *

January 15th, 1904
He is known as the Rabbi, though if he had ever been one, that fact is lost in the distant past. He is a noted

criminal, a man of arcane learning and appetites who evokes unsavoury stories from those who knew him. He is not one of us, yet he could be sympathetic to our cause…I would…with my life, but can I trust him with all of our lives?

I shall…tomorrow.

* * *

September 3rd, 1897
Were I to sum up the Basle Congress in one word— which I shall guard against pronouncing publicly—it would be this: at Basle I have founded the Jewish state. If I said this out loud today, I would be answered by universal laughter. Perhaps in five years, certainly in fifty, everyone will know it. The foundation of a State lies in the will of the people for a State.

* * *

From a transcript of an interview conducted by A. (a scrawled footnote in blue ink indicates he is a possible member of Mossad, Israel's secret service) with a man identified as The Rabbi (R). Some lines are unintelligible due to water damage.
A: How did it start?
R: I was living in Paris at the time. (Pause). You know what I was doing there.
A: I'm not sure I do. I understood you were running some sort of a gambling scheme to do with illegal ring fights?

R: That's essentially correct.

A: There were wild stories at the time that you were using golems. (Laughs).

R: (Laughs).

A: Did you know him?

R: We've met before.

A: I was not aware of that. Under what circumstances?

R: (Unintelligible)

A: So he trusted you.

R: I wouldn't say that. (Pause). No, he didn't trust me. But he had no choice.

* * *

The following comes from a microfilm of a notebook marked RABBI'S JOURNAL, *January 16th, 1904.*

A cold, clear day. I walked along the left bank in the early morning fog, watching the Seine. Notre Dame looked monstrous in the morning, like an ogre in the process of turning into stone. The place had a slimy, organic feel to it. I'd often wondered if it could be reanimated. Or per-haps it was constructed as a sort of uncompleted golem, left disused at the last moment before the placing of the *shem*.

By the time I arrived at the bookshop, the sun was fully formed in the sky and some of the fog had dis-persed. I was about to open the door when I noticed a coach had drawn to a halt a little further from me. Steam rose from the horses' nostrils as though they had been driven hard to come here.

I recognised him as soon as he stepped off the coach. He stepped briskly, though his eyes were tired and there was a gauntness about him. I said nothing. We didn't speak, then.

I opened the door and he followed me inside. I sat him down and prepared tea. The shop was cold in the mornings. I lit the oven and waited for the warmth to spread.

"You have been to Africa before," he said, breaking the silence at last. He was always a direct man.

"Your information is always reliable," I said.

"What were you doing there?"

"Do you not know?"

"Tell me."

I put cinnamon and honey into the teapot and stirred slowly, the way you stir old memories. "I followed that ass, Stanley," I said reluctantly.

"That was, what, in 1871?"

"I don't remember exactly."

"That was quite a journey. I recall reading about it. Seven hundred miles into the interior and back?"

"I was younger then."

And Stanley had his porters, all two hundred of them, while I walked behind, unseen and with nothing but myself to keep me alive. Stanley even had porters to carry his big brass bath for him. I washed in streams and in the rain, or didn't wash at all.

"Were you there since?"

"A few times."

"Where?"

"Zanzibar, the east coast." I poured the steaming tea into two mugs and added sugar. "I was with the Zulus in the Second Boer War."

"What were you doing?"

"I was studying with an *Inyanga*. Look, is this leading somewhere? I have a business to run."

He laughed. "Not many book buyers this time of the morning by the looks of it."

"What do you want?"

"I hear the shop has a basement connected to the catacombs," he said.

"You heard wrong."

"So you're out of the fights?"

I sipped my tea. I didn't like him coming to find me. I had not expected to see him again. I kept quiet, and I waited.

"I want you to go back to Africa," he said.

"Why?"

And then he told me.

* * *

The goal of our present endeavours must not be the "Holy Land," but a land of our own. We need nothing but a large piece of land for our poor brothers; a piece of land which shall remain our property from which no foreign master can expel us.

— *Leo Pinsker, Auto-Emancipation, 1882*

* * *

A: He mentioned Africa.

R: Yes. He seemed well-informed regarding my history there. But then, he was always well-informed.

A: Did he say what he wanted?

R: Not straight away. He led up to it. He talked a lot about politics.

A: What did he say?

R: He talked about the Russian pogroms. He felt there was a desperate need to find a place for the Jews of Russia, as they were under threat. (Pause). He wanted a homeland for the Jews.

A: But not Palestine?

R: I understood it wasn't feasible at the time. He mentioned negotiating with the Turkish Sultan. There was mention of land in Mesopotamia, Syria and Anatolia, but Palestine was excluded.

A: What else?

R: Cyprus. South Africa. America. He had given up on the Sultan. He was looking to the English for help. They were also talking about El Arish, in Egypt. (Unintelligible). He was working his way to it slowly.

A: Uganda?

R: It never was Uganda. That was a misconception from the start.

* * *

From the Rabbi's Journal, January 16th, 1904—Continued

"They're offering British East Africa," he said. "I had

meetings with Chamberlain, the Colonial Secretary. They're willing to grant us land there."

My tea had cooled on the table. The room felt warmer. Ancient books piled up on the floor and leaned against the wall. The sun scraped weakly against the grimy windows. I thought about Africa, about the heat that becomes a part of you, the smell it has, and of watching that endless blue sky and the smoke rising from distant human dwellings. I didn't want to admit to him I missed it.

"He told me the part he mentioned was on very high ground, with fine climate and every possibility for a great colony, one that could support at least a million souls."

"Where, exactly?"

He shrugged. "The Uasin Gishu Plateau."

He saw my look. Returned it. "It's on the border with Uganda, in the Kenya Province. I don't really know more than that." He paused and put his hands palms down on the table. "It's why I came to you."

"I don't know anything about it either," I said.

"But you could find out. You could go there."

I laughed. He looked at me with eyes whose calmness hid behind it a storm. "This is threatening to divide the Congress," he said quietly. "In fact, it *has* divided the congress. There are those who will settle for nothing less than Palestine. But, for now at least, this is a real possibility. An opportunity. I won't let it go past. Not lightly."

"Send your own people," I said. "I am not a surveyor."

He smiled. His fingers drummed a little on the table-top. "We will be sending out a small expedition. An *official* expedition. To survey the land, to evaluate its suitability. To bring back a detailed and public report."

I waited.

"Then there's you."

"What do you want me to do?"

And he grinned at that, because he knew he had successfully hooked me.

* * *

A: So he wanted you to go to East Africa.

R: Yes.

A: And you agreed.

R: Not at first. I told him to (unintelligible).

A: You didn't say that.

R: What did you expect? He came out of nowhere, out of the past, to ask me for a favour I didn't want to give. He had a lot of nerve.

A: But you agreed to do it. (Pause). You agreed to go.

R: (A long silence). Yes.

A: Did he tell you who else would be going?

R: No. He didn't know at that point. I was not to deal with him directly any more. All he gave me was one name.

A: Who was that?

R: Leopold Greenberg.

* * *

[The proposal to settle Jews in East Africa] is monstrous, extravagant, and unconstitutional, and opposed not only to the best interests of Christendom but of civilization at large.

– *E. Haviland Burke, M.P., parliamentary debate, 1904*

* * *

From the Rabbi's Journal, January 16th, 1904—Continued

I watched him go. He walked with his shoulders straight and his head high, poised like a man looking further ahead than anyone else I had ever known. But he moved slowly and he looked tired as he climbed into the coach. I watched him disappear into the traffic. He had given me one name.

"What do you need me for?" I had said.

"Think of it as backup," he said. "Of a...*spiritual* kind."

He was not a man given to talk of spirituality. He had a practical mind-set.

So did I.

"Leopold Greenberg will be organising the expedition. He is a British Jew. He was instrumental in our talks with the Colonial Office. You will communicate with him. He will make the official arrangements and pick the men. He will be your contact."

"Where will I find him?"

His fingers were splayed on the table. His skin looked brittle, like a page from an old bible.

"In Basle," he said. "It all comes back to Basle. He will contact you once he has made the preparations."

"The Congress," I said. He nodded. "This is splitting us up," he admitted. "But it might be our only option. When the time comes, you will know what to do."

When he was gone, I returned to the shop. Now, as I sit at the table writing this, I am filled with premonition. I am wary of his plans. And yet...I would be glad to see Africa again, and hear the elephant herds calling in the distance, and feel the warmth of a fire against my palms, and taste the smell of wood smoke. There are mysteries enough in Africa for a man's lifetime.

* * *

A: When did you get the call?

R: It came in November. It was snowing in Paris.

A: What did it say?

R: It was a summons. He was already dead by then. But Greenberg (unintelligible).

A: So what did you do?

R: (A long pause). I went to Basle.

* * *

From the Rabbi's Journal, 25th December, 1904
Basle was wrapped in a cold blanket of snow, and all the windows were lit from inside. Christmas Day, and I thought of red blood on white snow and hoped it was too cold for pogroms.

The death of the king. That is what it was about.

Renewal. As the year closes, the new year needs to be brought in, to be teased and tempted and conjured out of the ashes of the old year, until the sun reappears and warmth and life return. He was dead now, since July, when he contracted pneumonia, swiftly, unexpectedly, and forever. But his essence still lived on, and I was still compelled by him, by ties I could not easily shake, and so I walked the cold streets of Basle and thought of him, and of a life that comes from death.

Greenberg was younger than I expected. He looked tired but pleased, like a man whose hard work was finally done. We sat in his small office. A map was spread on the table before us.

"I just got out of the committee meeting," he said. "We signed the contract. The expedition is leaving tomorrow." He fiddled with a pen. On the map, mountains and valleys, rivers and lakes were reduced to lines of ink. "I want you to leave with them."

I nodded. I had brought a small bag with me and was ready to leave. I had closed off my operations in Paris for the time being. The shop, too. It never had too many customers. The basement was full of the immobile statues of mythical creatures designed to fight, now peaceful.

"There are three men," he said. "Major Alfred St. Hill Gibbons will lead the expedition. He's an old Africa hand."

I nodded. I had read his *Through the Heart of Africa from South to North*. He was a well-known explorer.

I dimly wondered if we'd met before, but decided we hadn't.

"The second man is Professor Alfred Kaiser, a Swiss. He's also had some experience in East Africa, and was a scientific advisor to the *North West Cameroons Co.*"

I waited.

"The third man is the only one of our own. We felt it was judicious to include at least one Jew in the expedition." He smiled. "Young Wilbusch. He's Russian, an engineer—comes from a family of Zionists. Never been to Africa before, though."

"There's always a first time," I said.

"Quite." He fell silent. Then, "This is important, Rabbi. More than you perhaps realise. The Russian Jews are being slaughtered. No one knows how long we have left in Europe before another wave of repression attempts to sweep us away. We're aliens here."

"You could say the same for wherever Jews go," I said. "You will be no less of an alien in East Africa."

"Perhaps," he said. "But to have one's own land—the way the French do, the way the Germans and the British and the Swiss do—that makes all the difference. A place to call your own. This place—this Uasin Gishu Plateau—it could become a Jewish homeland, the first in two thousand years. We need to know." He laughed; it was a tired sound. "What we *really* need is a good report back. Anything else will kill the Uganda Plan." He saw my expression and shrugged. "I know it's not Uganda, but that's what everyone is calling it. The Uganda Plan.

I don't care. Let them call it what they will, as long as the report is favourable and the British carry it through. We need a miracle."

"I don't do miracles," I said. He laughed. "I've arranged tickets for you, money and as much as I know of Gibbons' itinerary, which is bound to change in response to circumstances."

I nodded. I took the documents and the money from him.

"There is a lot of hostility to the idea of a Jewish colony in East Africa," he said. "Particularly amongst the white farmers already there. They're calling it Jewganda. You might have to watch out in case they try anything."

"You want me to act as a bodyguard to the expedition?"

"Oh, no," he said hurriedly. "I'm sure Gibbons is capable of taking care of things. Nevertheless…"

"Yes."

"Spiritual backup."

"Right."

When we bid each other farewell with a handshake he smiled again, wistfully, and said, "I wish I could go with them. With you."

"I will see you in two months," I said, and stepped into the cold outside. He closed the door behind me without speaking further.

I'm sitting in my hotel room writing this, while the snow beats against the window and it seems as though the new year will never come, that the old year's corpse will remain frozen on the ground until there is nothing left alive. Morbid thoughts; I would be glad to leave Europe again.

* * *

To read of this beautiful land of perennial streams and no fevers being reserved for foreign Jewish paupers is enough to make one wish for a big nose and a name like Ikey Moses.

— *Letter to the* African Standard, *November 19th, 1904.*

* * *

A: So then you left Basle.

R: In the morning. I went to Trieste.

A: That's where the ship left from.

R: Right. The *S.S. Africa.*

A: Did you meet the others?

R: I saw them. Greenberg showed me photographs so I could recognise them. Gibbons, Kaiser, and Wilbusch. But I didn't make any contact with them. Not then.

A: How long did the journey take?

R: You know all this. Why do you keep asking me these questions?

A: Humour me.

R: (A long pause). Two and a half weeks.

A: To Mombassa?

R: To Mombassa.

A: Tell me about Wilbusch.

R: (Unintelligible).

* * *

The following is from a microfilm of the book published by Wertheimer, Lea and Co., of London, in 1905:
Report on the work of the commission sent out to examine the territory offered by H.M. Government to the Zionist Organization for the purposes of a Jewish settlement in British East Africa.
This extract is from Wilbusch's diary.
1904
December

24 Berlin
Started by Basle Express.

25 Basle
Arrived. Present at Committee Meeting. Contract signed.

26 Milan
Left Basle at 7 o'clock in the morning by express. Arrived at Milan 3 o'clock in the afternoon. Saw sights of the town. Left by Venice Express in the evening.

27 Venice
Saw the sights. Left in the evening by Trieste Express
.

28 Trieste
Received Theodolite through the post. Embarked on

board *S.S. Africa* at 4 o'clock in the afternoon.

29-31 Adriatic Sea
Continuation of voyage on board *S.S. Africa*.

1905
January

1 Mediterranean
Continuation of voyage.

2 Port Said
Voltameter, etc., received through post. Passed through
Suez Canal.

3 Suez and Gulf of Suez
Continued voyage from Port Said to Aden. 1,397 knots

4-5 Red Sea
Continuation of voyage.

7 Aden
Arrived in the morning. Re-embarked in the evening.

8-12 Indian Ocean
Continuation of voyage.

12 Kilindini
Arrived in Kilindini in the afternoon (the port before

Mombassa—from Aden to Mombassa, 1,611 nautical miles).

13 Mombassa
Day 86°F. Hot and sultry. Left the boat in the morning.

* * *

From the Rabbi's Journal, January 14th, 1905
The heat was like an old, comfortable hat, misplaced for some time but not lost. The old year had departed, the new year had come, and the sun did rise again. Here, it had never set.

Low European houses stretched inland from the harbour. In the distance you could hear the whistle of a train, the voices of porters from the harbour and of sellers in the market. Yet, compared to Europe, it was quiet; there was a stillness in the air, and a sense of massive distances, of a gulf that had been growing as we crossed the ocean until it stretched across half the world and now separated us from everything we knew.

I observed Wilbusch this morning, following behind as he and Kaiser strolled through the market and Gibbons was kept busy elsewhere, engaging a headman, personal servants, and porters for the journey ahead. Wilbusch has been quiet, and seems a little overawed by his experience, though he tries to hide it. I do not think he and Gibbons get along very well.

I am writing this on the train. The expedition had boarded what they call the Uganda Railway—the train to Nairobi—and I followed them. They have ten porters with them. We are passing the Kaptu and Athi plains as I write this. There are numerous herds of antelopes and zebra outside.

* * *

From Wilbusch's diary
1905
January

16 Nairobi
Day 85° F. 9 p.m. 72°. Bearable heat.
    Went with Mr. Kaiser to see Mr. Marcus. In the afternoon saw town and market with Mr. Kaiser and Mr. Marcus, and had a long conversation.

* * *

From Major A. St. H. Gibbons' report (Wertheimer, Lea and Co., 1905)
Caravans composed entirely of up-country boys frequently proved unreliable, and by desertion or perversity might subject the Commission to serious delays—a risk which, having a view to the limited time at our disposal, I did not feel disposed to take. At Nairobi I engaged a further thirty-five porters, and all arrangements were completed in time to catch the first train westward, leaving on the morning of the second day after our arrival.

* * *

From the Rabbi's Journal, January 16th, 1905
Following them, I am struck by how different the three
men are. First, there is Gibbons: a bluff, hearty man,
used to command, British to his core, a man at the apex
of humanity, for whom all others are by default sub-
ordinate. Not a bad choice for leader, but I can see he
and Wilbusch, if they hadn't done so, would clash. Wilbusch: pale (though his skin will soon tan in this African
sun), a little frightened. There is little he recognises here,
and once we are past Nakuru and the farmlands...

Kaiser, the Swiss, is cool and composed. He gets along
well with both, but seems more interested in his instru-
ments. The three are surrounded by porters and servants
until it sometimes seems they are going not on a voyage
of exploration but one of colonization; they could start
a nation of their own, or one each and fight amongst
themselves.

The thought makes me smile as I observe them. We
are waiting in Nakuru, a small town with a railway station and not much else. There appears to have been a
delay with some of their equipment. Meanwhile, Gibbons has sent the porters ahead to prepare their base
camp. From here on, we will be entering the Uasin
Gishu territory.

* * *

From Wilbusch's Diary
1905
January

17 Nairobi-Nakuru

Conversation in the morning with Mr. Marcus and the Jewish farmers—Messrs. Solsky and Bloch. Started 11 a.m. on the Uganda Railway; passed the Kikuyu territory, the only locality where we saw a numerous population and fertile agricultural land. Reached Nakuru at 7:30 p.m. Our luggage left behind in Nairobi.

18 Nakuru (448 miles)

Day 75° F. Evening and mornings about 52° F. 5 p.m. Moderate rain.

Kept waiting because of the absence of luggage and scarcity of porters. Visited the mountains with Mr. Kaiser in the morning, and the Njoro River, where the water fluctuations could be observed in the afternoon.

19 Nakuru

4-7 p.m. Rain.

Again kept waiting on account of absence of luggage and scarcity of porters. Visited Njoro River with Mr. Kaiser in the afternoon.

20 Nakuru

Kept waiting on account of scarcity of porters. Luggage received and tent pitched.

21 Nakuru

Kept waiting on account of scarcity of porters.

* * *

A: Tell me about the journey into the territory.

R: I knew where their base camp was, so I didn't follow directly. It was forty-one miles from Nakuru to the Eldoma Ravine. There were some Jewish farmers there, mainly South Africans who heard of the plan and were eager for it to succeed. I stayed with one of them, London, after they had stayed with him. I...ran some tests.

A: What sort of tests?

R: I'm not sure you'd understand.

A: Try me.

R: I took a measurement of the—the *feeling*, you could say, of the place. There is a way to (unintelligible) the vibrations of the *sephirot*.

A: What did you find?

R: Nothing I could put my finger on, at the time. Something odd. Like a place that is familiar though you've never been there before? But also, like a place that was *more* than once place, as if the sephirot somehow overlapped there. Reminds you a little of Safed. We call it a place close to the skies. (Laughs). You can call it mumbo-jumbo.

A: Did you speak to this farmer? London?

R: A little. I understood Wilbusch had a long conversation with him the night before. London said he got the impression Wilbusch was a little out of his depth—also that he did not get along with the Major.

A: Did he say what their mood was? Regarding the

expedition?

R: It was still in the early days. We hadn't even reached the territory proper yet. I'd say they were cautiously optimistic, but there were some concerns.

A: What were they?

R: Wilbusch was worried about water. Kaiser about arable land. I think Gibbons was mainly worried about more practical aspects—namely, being attacked by a local tribe. I know he arranged for some guns—some Snider rifles—and also some Masai guides through Foaker, the Collector of the district.

A: Tell me about the approach to the territory.

R: (Unintelligible).

* * *

From Gibbons' report

The ravine station, which stands on top of a small steep hill four miles north of the Equator, has an altitude of some 7,000 feet above sea level and commands a magnificent view of the Kamasia range of mountains, over which we were about to travel *en route* for the plateau beyond. These mountains are almost entirely covered with dense primeval forest and extend from the south-eastern corner of the prospective territory, first in an easterly, then in a northerly direction. A well-cut path, suitable for pedestrian traffic only, leads for the first day's journey through a belt of undulating and rapidly rising forest land similar in character to that surmounting the Elgeyo escarpment, which forms the eastern boundary line of the suggested settlement. Amid the great entanglement of rope-like vines, creepers, giant thistles, and other underscrub, huge trees—some of them many feet in diameter—rise to a height of eighty feet and upwards.

* * *

From Wilbusch's Diary
1905
January

28
Camp in territory between Nesoi and Kinjuno (about 0°7' N lat. 35°35' E long.)
    5.30 a.m. 43° F. 3 p.m. 72° F. 9 p.m. 54° F. 8 p.m. Rain.
    Marched about 10 miles NNW: almost the whole of the road through dry and desert plains. Traces of small trees and bamboo. No timber, no pasturage, no game, no people. Only one spring, at the fourth mile.

29
In the territory.

* * *

From the Rabbi's Journal, January 29th
The land changes as I move through it, over it. In the distance I can see smoke rising from camp fires, but otherwise there is no sign of humanity. I am camped in the forest while they are camped nearby, near the source of

the Samabula River.

It is a beautiful land. A man could become lost here and live the rest of his life as a nomad and not see enough of this place. The forest spreads away from me, dark and full of secrets. The undergrowth whispers in a language I can almost understand. Some of these trees are ancient, their spirits slumbering inside the vast trunks. I do not dare awake them. There was fog in the morning—Africa is at its most beautiful in the morning, when the fog wreaths the hills in crowns and the sun begins to open, like a flower, across the horizon. The place is teeming with invisible life. Animals live a secret life in the forest, and I have seen the prints of elephants and zebras and lions. It is like coming home.

I feel as if Paris never existed. Basle, London, all the cold and dreary cities of Europe disappear, and all that remains is this vast expanse of land, open to the skies, the trees its arms and the rivers its arteries. I fear for this place, I realise; if we came here we would cut the trees for timber and houses, and we would chain up the rivers to power our factories, and we would hunt down the lions and keep the zebras in a zoo. Something of this already lies, superimposed, on the land beyond my eyes. when I close them I think I can see it, this old-new land of Herzl's, this *Altneuland*.

I have hunted for hare and, having eaten, I write this in the light of the fire. They won't see me from their camp, though I think the Masai suspect my presence. Tomorrow, I think, the expedition will split up, and each will go in a different direction.

So will I.

* * *

From Wilbusch's diary
1905
January
30

Dispatched the mail in the morning. 22 men went to the ravine. Took surveys of the mountains with the Theodolite in the forenoon. At 3 o'clock in the afternoon I separated with 10 men for 6 days. I have drawn up this small itinerary at the request of Major Gibbons, for the latter said that we ought to meet at the end of that time on the Sirgoi to proceed from there to the Elgon. Went 4 miles NNW, saw a few antelope in a valley. Nothing but dry grass plains all round. No water.

* * *

A: Which way did you go?
R: I skirted the forest, searching for open land. I was looking for the Moguan.
A: The Moguan?

* * *

If we consider the Guas Ngishu [Uasin Gishu] Plateau with regard to its native population, we must point out, as already remarked, that the greater portion of the territory is at present without any population. It has,

however, been populated…we find unmistakable traces of population—that is to say, circular stone walls with an inner diameter of 2 to 40 metres, which partly represent ruins of huts, but partially also fortifications in the shape of circular walls. In many places, the Masai of today call these stone erections "Moguan." They are 2 metres in height and 1 metre in thickness. They are built of quarry stones, carefully fitted into each other …Not infrequently, the roughly wattled huts of Wandorobo hunters, who consumed their booty there and heaped up enormous quantities of bones, are found in these depressions. In many cases these Moguan are also made of large rocks placed in a circle, and must then be considered as the defences or so-called "Bomas" of the vanished population. I have seen similar stone erections in Southern Kavirondo and on the heights of the Mau Mountains, and I know that they are found in Nandi, also. It may therefore be supposed that all those Moguan have their origin in an ancient population…
– *From Dr. Alfred Kaiser's Report (Wertheimer, Lea and Co., 1905)*

* * *

A: Why were you looking for these Moguan?
R: (Unintelligible).

* * *

From the Rabbi's Journal, February 4th
As I close my eyes, the landscape is still visible to

me—*more* visible to me—but it is no longer singular. It is like watching a picture through lenses that refract and overlap the image, until it resembles a hazy mosaic. Yet it *is* becoming clearer to me—the source of the interference, of the overlap, as if time has been piled onto time, and I see one layer as the present and another as the future, or the past. Or perhaps I am only watching two different presents…

Today I walked through open grass plains. There were herds of antelope in the distance, and I thought I had heard a lion, though I couldn't see it. My skin is turning brown in this sun; I have discarded most of my European clothing and now walk with my upper body bare, as well as my feet, the soles of which are gradually growing hard again. During my short time in the forest I had gathered several rare herbs and tree barks. At midday, I stopped in the shade of an acacia and built a small fire, and made a tea with some of the herbs I had gathered.

When I drank it the world became clearer, the picture I had been carrying in my head since arriving became focused. The Moguan shine in this mental landscape like pinpricks of light, like the points on the Tree of Life. They seem to form a pattern whose meaning I cannot yet see. Later, when it cools down, I will continue my journey. I am near to one of them, can feel it, its vibrations—it is a source of power. I think they are like the holes made by a needle in a cloth, the points the thread passes through when it binds one material to another.

February 5th

I have come across a Nandi hunting party this morning, camped in the Moguan I was seeking yesterday. The Moguan is a large, circular structure made of great stone walls, somewhat resembling an eye planted in the earth. I walked through an opening into the confines of this eye, which is like an imposing courtyard open to the sky. The Nandi hunters surrounded me, looking wary. They were armed with spears and some European guns, which they levelled at me.

I spoke to them in Swahili, which several of them spoke. They had with them an old *Inyanga*—I am using the Zulu word here, and I think their word for what we may call *tzaddik* is *Orkoiyot*, though I cannot be sure— who came forward and put his hand on my forehead. I could feel the power in him, and for a moment we stood in perfect stillness. Once more I could feel the dual nature of this land swim against the back of my eyes, growing clearer all the while. Then the Inyanga released me and smiled, and the rest of the Nandi removed their weapons.

"You are far from home, *mzungu*," he said. Mzungu means "White man" in Swahili. There was a puzzled look in his eyes when he spoke.

"What is home?" I said, and he laughed. He invited me to their fire, and I shared in their food. Antelope meat was cooking on the coals.

I am convinced that the Nandi are connected to this mystery I can feel here. They are remarkably Semitic in appearance, and when I spoke to their healer by the fire he said their forefathers—whom he called Kalenjin— had travelled South over the centuries, coming from a place by a great river in a hot and arid desert, which I take to mean Egypt. They practice circumcision—as I found out when several of us relieved ourselves after sharing water—and believe in God, whom they call *Asis*. I spoke for long with the healer, but it is what we did not speak of—the shades that walk over this earth as if they are real—that underlined our conversation.

At last, he offered to let me join them. He was as curious about me as I was about him, I think. I had given him some of the herbs I had collected, receiving in return a small store of dried powder that he said contained the power of vision. We shall travel together— both here and, I hope, in that other place.

I have not lost sight of the others, but they have all gone in different directions. I have a feeling Wilbusch will become lost...

* * *

A: What do you mean they are Semitic?

R: What didn't you understand?

A: They're black.

R: So are the Ethiopian Jews. The Falash Mura. You could argue they, and not European Jews, are the true descendants of Israel. King Solomon –

A: If you're talking about the Queen of Sheba –

R: I don't rightly know if you have any idea what I'm

talking about.

A: (Pause.) I'm trying to understand.

R: What is the purpose of all this questioning? This all took place a long time ago. It's barely a footnote to history. The Uganda Plan. A barely-remembered story. Why do you suddenly care?

A: (Unintelligible).

* * *

From Wilbusch's diary
1905
February

6 Camp on the Sirgoi
6 a.m. 52° F. 4 p.m. 80° F. 9 p.m. 60° F. During the day strong east winds. Evening calm.

Waited for main caravan. Made map of the route. Went about 3 miles south during the afternoon, but found no one. Territory: the same moderately good pasture grass, but a little more dry; no water or wood anywhere; many antelope.

7 On the Sirgoi
6 a.m. 42° F. 12 noon 84° F. 5 p.m. 79° F. 9 p.m. 52° F. Strong east wind during the day. Clear. Evening calm. Waited for main caravan and wrote preliminary report. Went about 2 miles south in the afternoon, then about 2 miles east, saw no one. The porters' rice came to an end today.

8 On the Sirgoi

6.30 a.m. 54° F. 2 p.m. 78° F. 9 p.m. 56° F. Strong east wind during the day. Evening quiet.

Waited for main caravan, but no one came.

* * *

From Gibbons' report

On February 8th I spent another tedious day in the forest. It took ten hours to make as many miles. Fortunately, in the late afternoon we emerged onto a narrow open strip about a mile in length, and here camp was pitched for the night. By noon the following day the forest was cleared, and about a mile further we passed the farm of three South Africans, the brothers Van Breda. Their oxen and donkeys were a living proof of the excellence of the pasture in their district. One of the brothers informed me that a few nights previously, three oxen had been stolen from the "kraal" adjoining the house. About a fortnight later, we heard that first the remaining cattle were stolen, and finally ten savages approached the boy who tended the donkeys within half a mile of the house, told him to go home, and proceeded to drive the donkeys into the forest. By the time the boy could apprise his masters of the robbery, the thieves had made good their escape, and an attempt to overtake them proved futile.

* * *

From the Rabbi's Journal, February 10th

I did not take part in the raid on the farm. The Nandi

hunters, who had been to the place several days previously, now returned to complete their acquisitions,
as it were. We went deep into the forest with the animals. Their village, they informed me, was at the foot-
hills of the Chipchangwane mountains to the north. As
we walked through the darkening forest, strange howls
could be heard in the distance of a kind I had not heard
before, being neither lion nor elephant nor any other
animal I could recognise. The Nandi seemed worried,
casting glances at the thick underbrush of the forest,
and kept their weapons at the ready. I asked the Inyanga
what it was.

"*Kerit,*" he said. He did not elaborate.

The others did not look happy at his mentioning the
name.

"Probably a lion," one of them, Wambua, said in Swahili. He did not look as though he believed it.

The animals, too, were frightened, and the hunters
had considerable problems getting them to move along.
At last we stopped on a rocky outcrop that overlooked
the entire valley below, spread open like a map. The
Nandi were easier here, and built a fire. That night we
were not disturbed, though the howls of the Kerit continued to be heard in the distance.

February 11th
I woke up in the night and, going to relive myself beyond
the boundaries of the camp, heard the howl of a Kerit
close by. I saw a large animal sitting up on its haunches

no more than thirty yards away. It was nearly five feet high and moved with a shambling gait. I shouted, and it stopped and turned its head to look at me. It was larger than a bear and as heavily built. The forequarters were very thickly furred, as were all four legs, and the head was long and pointed and resembled a bear's. Somehow, there was a sense of the primate about it, too, and its eyes held mine for a long moment before it disappeared into the forest. It had not harmed me.

I returned to the camp and found the Inyanga waiting by the fire, looking grave. "What is a Kerit?" I said.

He made a sign with his hand, as if warding off evil, but then seemed to relax. "Our people say it is a devil which prowls on the darkest nights, seeking people, especially children, to devour. It is half like a man and half like a huge, ape-faced bird, and you may know it at once from its fearful howling roar, and because in the dark of night its mouth glows red like the embers of a log."

I waited, recognising some of what he said in the animal I saw, but doubting its evil. "And what do *you* say?" I asked at last.

He smiled. He had many teeth missing. "It is an animal," he said. "I have heard the European settlers call it the Nandi Bear, but I have never seen a bear, and the Nandi do not claim this animal as ours."

"I have never seen such an animal," I said, but then a dim memory rose in my mind, of a visit to a museum, a long time ago on another continent, under another name. There was a skeleton on display. The Inyanga nodded as if reading my mind.

"Tomorrow my people will return to their village," he said. "But, if you are willing, not you and I." He stirred the embers with a stick and sighed. The night was very still. "This land is both old and new," he said, and I was again reminded of Herzl's words, of *Altneuland*. "What we call the past and the future are, perhaps, not as firmly fixed in their positions as they should be. I will show you."

"Show me what?" I said.

"The place where the Kerit live," he said.

He said no more, and shortly returned to his sleep. I find myself unable to follow. I sit and write by the dying light of the fire.

Tomorrow, then.

* * *

A: What is this *Kerit*?

R: I had thought it a—what is the term we use today?—an endangered species. (Laughs). The creature I saw that night looked powerful, but not malevolent. I think it is only humans who can be evil, while animals only follow their nature. Is that old fashioned?

A: But what is it? There are no bears in Africa.

R: When I returned, I went back to the museum I remembered. I saw the same skeleton. It was…similar. It could have been the same animal, or at least is forefather.

A: What was it?

R: A Chalicothere. (Pause.) A species of perissodactyl mammals that evolved in the mid-Eocene, around forty million years ago (pause). They died out three and a half million years ago.

* * *

From Gibbons' Report

On the morning of the 11th I climbed the hill to the west, on the lower slopes of which my camp stood, and from the summit commanded a comprehensive view of the country around me. To the north a bold, rough country presented itself to my view. A great group of mountains lay back for many miles, many of these appearing to attain an altitude of 10,000 to 12,000 feet. Some were abrupt and rugged, some of gentler gradient. A few were covered, or partially covered, with dense forest, though the majority grew grass, except where the rock bed was exposed. To the northeast and east there appeared to be an interminable stretch of primeval forest, interspersed at rare intervals with small patches of grassland. I saw at once that any attempt to make my way in that direction was out of the question. It would have required much more time than I had at my disposal. I determined, therefore, to skirt the range on its western boundary. A very rough commencement led us for some 700 feet down the steep slopes of the hill into a rugged valley below. Tracing a stream with clear mountain water, we finally entered a narrow valley girt on all sides by mountains and extending upwards of fifteen miles to the north. This valley might well be called "Valley of the Lions." I never heard so many of these animals in any one place as I did during the two nights I was encamped here.

* * *

From the Rabbi's Journal, February 12th
This morning the Nandi departed with their loot, heading for lower ground, and the Inyanga and I headed north and up the mountains. We came across what appeared to be Gibbons' camp. There were signs there of much movement, and the Inyanga, upon examining the ground, chuckled.

"His guide is Masai," he said, "and ignorant of this land. There has been a mutiny, of sorts. No doubt the porters were afraid to head further north for fear of the Nandi. But I can see the Mzungu chief overruled them, for they have continued on their way."

We reached a stream and I washed myself in its cool water, and swam. The water was sweet and, standing still in the water, I caught fish with my fingers. The Inyanga put sharpened stakes through them and we grilled them on a small fire. It seemed Gibbons was heading in the same direction as we were, and the Inyanga thought it prudent not to follow too quickly. At night I heard the Kerit again, far in the distance. When I raised my head the stars filled the entire sky, and the Milky Way was exposed like a rich vein of diamonds revealed in the wall of a dark mine.

The Inyanga and I prepared a tea with the dark bark of a tall evergreen tree that grows here on the mountain. The tea made me drowsy, but behind my eyes the lands, their disparity, grew closer, and I began to imagine I could see streets, wide avenues lined with trees, and unknown automobiles moving along the paved roads, as slow as snails since there were so many of them. Globes of electrical lights hung high above the street, and the air was full of an unfamiliar stench, like that of chemical smoke pouring out of an invisible factory. I saw the stream, but in my dream it was no longer filled with water but with a sort of inky greyness in which nothing lived. Somewhere in the distance I heard an explosion, and a car with a red star of David painted on its side sped past me, but was soon halted by the traffic. I heard people scream.

I shook myself with difficulty away from the dream. For a long time I sat by the brook and stared into the water and listened to the silence.

* * *

From Wilbusch's Diary
1905
February

13 Base camp
Waited on account of scarcity of porters. At 6 o'clock in the morning 19 men went to the ravine for rice. About 5 in the afternoon Mr. Kaiser went NW to the Nzoia

with 14 men. I remained with 8 men in the camp. Made sketch of the route.

14 Base camp

Kept waiting for want of porters. Made excursion of about 3½ miles to Karuna with Masia and one porter. On the third mile I took specimens of the soil and minerals from Karuna, which consisted of quartz rock and stone. Ascended to the summit. The view was little pleasing, except the Elgeyo escarpment, which was wooded. There was inferior and dried-up pasture grass everywhere. No water and no trees. To the north there were the Akkabrie Mountains, the slopes of which were dotted with isolated bushes. No trace of life or of people. On the road the grass is short and drying. Several antelope, water-bucks and hares. At the second mile, and on the top of Karuna, were stone kraals which had been abandoned a long time.

15 Base camp

Read "The Uganda Protectorate" by Sir. H. Johnson. Delayed owing to want of porters.

16 Base camp

Waited owing to want of porters.

* * *

From the Rabbi's Journal, February 17th

The Chipchangwane Mountains make for a slow ascent,

yet from their height the whole of the Uasin Gishu Plateau can be seen below, and it is a magnificent sight. When I look at it normally it is a land of wide savannahs and green mountains, rolling brooks and flowing streams, of herds of elephants and darting hare. Yet when I close my eyes it metamorphoses, and it is a land of white stone and paved roads, of factories and smoke. Small, black dirigibles float in the air where, when my eyes are open, only clouds exist.

Electric light brings day to the plateau even on a moonless night, and the silence is replaced with a constant din of engines and people, construction, and occasional unexplained bursts of gunfire and distant explosions that send clouds of smoke into the sky. I am disturbed by it, but when I ask the Inyanga he smiles serenely and talks of the past being the future and the future the past.

We began our descent today, and the plateau, not entirely to my regret, is disappearing from view. We seem still to be following in Gibbons' steps, though he is long gone from here. In the course of our journey we have several times stopped and spent the night in abandoned Moguan. There, the power of the vision is strongest, and when I drink from the tea and close my eyes, I can see the stone walls grow and reach up to the skies, and close above my head. There are vast buildings made entirely of white stone, a whole new Jerusalem, and the Moguan are only their worn-down remains, like the bleached bone skeleton of a dinosaur.

I can hear the Kerit in the distance, howling at the
night sky. I saw one last night, moving away. It is almost
as if they are following us.

February 19th
We are in a narrow valley, with mountains rising on
either side of it, as imposing and constrictive as the
walls of a synagogue. What are we doing here? I have
seen a herd of Kerit moving down below. The Inyanga
led me further down. We followed a small river to a
rocky enclave, where it disappeared underground. The
Inyanga entered the water and motioned for me to do
the same. I felt like a fish with nothing but my skin, no
possessions and no burdens; a dark fish swimming in a
clear calm world.

We went through the fissure in the rock and tumbled
down a waterfall into a cave. The water continued to
flow onward and disappeared into the earth. The cave
was small and dark, but the Inyanga motioned for me
to follow him and we went through a crack in the rock
and...

* * *

A: Did the Kerit try to harm you?
R: No. But I noticed several of them sit still on their
haunches and stare at us. I had a feeling then that they
could communicate if they wanted to. A feeling of intelligence. However, I never found out for sure. I also felt...
(pause). I suspect they were there for a reason. Almost

as if they were guarding that hidden valley, or rather, guarding what was inside it. But I don't know.
A: What was in the cave?

* * *

From the Rabbi's Journal, February 20th
I had to stop writing rather abruptly yesterday. We were in a giant cavern deep under the earth. Yesterday, leaving the cave, we traversed a long way through tunnels of hard rock. There was a whole maze of caves down here, and had it not been for the Inyanga I would have been lost within minutes. The darkness was pure, but as we descended further and the air grew warm, the walls began to glow with a faint light that came from a kind of moss or fungus growing on them. No doubt Kaiser would have been most interested to examine them, had he been here.

I began to find debris littering the floors. Curious things: a burnt toy automobile of a shape and material I had never seen before; a broken disc made of a material slightly resembling Parkesine that even in the faint light reflected, when turned, the whole rainbow of colours; an elongated gun with a button instead of a trigger. Here and there, too, I saw rusting plaques on those cold stone walls, the script adorning them all but faded away. It was as if the place had suffered some instantaneous, unexpected holocaust that had removed all persons but left some of their effects behind. Yet there was also the sense of a kind of timelessness, or of some distant age buried under aeons.

At last our route came to an end. We stood in a small cave, deep within the earth. The walls, covered in moss, seemed to breathe. They cast an eerie glow over a small pool of water that rested in the middle of the cave, and which we approached.

The Inyanga knelt down by the pool, and I followed him. "Do not drink from it," he warned. "Look only."

I looked into the water. I...

February 22nd

I did something foolish. Let me tell it from the beginning.

The Inyanga and I were in the cave. I looked into the water.

Uasin Gishu was spread before me.

The whole of the plateau appeared to me in the water, as if I were a bird looking down from up high. Ringed by mountains, the terrain was otherwise changed beyond recognition.

Roads criss-crossed the plateau. They were two- and three-lane roads, and yet they were chock full with traffic. It consisted entirely of motorcars, of types and makes I have never seen. One resembled the toy car I had seen in the tunnels. The rivers were polluted and dead, each harnessed to fantastic factories that sat squarely on the banks. Beyond them, from Chipchangwane to the peaks of Nandi and Kavirondo, the land was a maze of architecture. Tall buildings, taller than anything save perhaps the towers in America, reached silver pinnacles towards the sun. It was a land of chrome and silver and glass, and amongst those constructions lay white-stone houses, whole towns of stones, like the numerous neigh-bourhoods of Jerusalem.

The view in the pool changed, became a hot, dusty street of pale stone. There were few people afoot, yet my attention was not on the travellers but on the shop signs: they were all in Hebrew.

I moved without thinking. "No!" the Inyanga said.

I shook him off; though he was old, he was still strong. "It is an illusion," he said, trying to dissuade me.

"It's real," I said, and I reached down to the water and cupped some in my hand, and drank it.

The Inyanga looked at me for a long moment, sadness etched into his lined face. "What will be, has been," he said, and those were the last words I heard. The drink of water had taken its effect on me, and I felt my body freeze, my muscles contracting, causing me to lose my purchase on the ground. I fell towards the pool.

My head hit water, and then the rest of my body fol-lowed. I felt a momentary sensation of drowning.

Then I was in the white-stone street, walking along towards one of the high-rising silver buildings. Over-head, aircraft flew—strange great things like silver bullets with wings—and here and there I could dis-cern the colourful bubbles of floating dirigibles. A car approached me at speed, the driver honking his horn and making me jump.

There were trees planted along the road, providing welcome shade, and the shops were all open and selling a variety of products that nearly spilled onto the pavement. I passed a greengrocer selling pineapples and bananas, fresh ripe corn and golden apples. It was followed by a bakery with magnificent cakes in the windows, and then by a shop selling brides' dresses, and another that sold spices. Café houses were dotted along the road and people sat at tables outside and drank small glasses of coffee, and ate cakes and smoked. The company was mixed, men and women together. All the shop signs were in Hebrew.

I saw a shop selling newspapers. They, too, were mostly in Hebrew, though there were newspapers there in English and French and Russian, too. I looked at some of the headlines but could make little sense of them, though they filled me with unease.

* * *

Uprising Will Be Crushed, Vows Chief-of-Staff.
Sources at the Weizmann Institute Report Successful Cloning of Saurian DNA.
President Einstein To Resign: Says War "Immoral."

* * *

My feet led me to a large square. Beyond it lay a quarter of silver and glass high-rising buildings.

I turned at the sound of many marching feet.

Through that hot, dusty haze a platoon of soldiers

came marching in true English style, legs rising and falling in rhythm, uniforms immaculate and on display. Their guns were long, sleek machines that seemed to purr as they were carried.

Behind the soldiers came huge vehicles, armour-plated with moving tracts for wheels and the long barrel of a cannon emerging from their turrets.

I heard a voice beside me and turned to see an elderly gentleman in a chequered shirt opened at the neck, a pair of ridiculous-looking trousers cut short at the knee, and a pair of biblical-looking sandals.

"Beautiful, aren't they?" he said, and there was a gleam in his eye. He spoke Hebrew to me, but with a strange, heavy accent that was a little that of the Dutch *Afrikaaners* and a little of Russian, too, perhaps. "I used to drive one of these when I was still in the army."

I became conscious of my nakedness then, afraid to draw attention to myself, but upon a cursory examination realised I was dressed in a similar way to my new friend, with the addition of a hat.

"The army?" I said. He chuckled as if I had said something funny. "Best army in the world," he said. "Everyone knows that. Ask the British, even."

He must have misinterpreted my expression. "Don't worry," he said reassuringly, laying his hand on my arm. "The Mau Mau are not a serious threat. We can deal with them."

I was about to speak when I felt someone was observing me, yet I could see no one but for my companion.

I bid him goodbye and walked away. The feeling persisted.

I came to a crowded place. Large, double-decker omnibuses stopped there, picking and letting off passengers. I saw an old *chasid*, dressed in black despite the heat, get onto one of the buses. Someone shouted. I turned, saw two men fight with the man in black. A scream.

The man exploded.

It must have been strapped to his body, under his clothes. The bomb ripped his body apart and blew out the windows of the bus. More screams filled the air. I saw a wounded woman crawl out of the bus with her left hand missing. I heard sirens. I smelled the mixed stench of smoke and blood.

It was like being in a dream, I thought, that had turned bad. I felt myself pulled away from the scene of carnage into a feeling of insubstantiality as I wandered through the streets in a haze that grew the more I walked, until I saw nothing but white walls, a white space turning dark blue as I fell into it, all the while feeling the unseen eyes burning into me…

I surfaced in the pool, inside the cave. The Inyanga was squatting above me, looking into the pool with the same expression of sadness on his face. I pulled myself out. When I looked into the water again the vision was gone, and with it the feeling I was being observed.

We didn't speak on our way out. I couldn't get over the feeling I had done something profoundly wrong.

* * *

From Gibbons' Report
On the 24th camp was pitched immediately to the west
of the mountains, near a small spring of good water. The
following day I sent boys out in different directions to try
and find the base camp, which according to my instruc-
tions was to have been pitched as close to the mountain
as water would allow. They returned without success, and
a climb to the top of the mountain, though it offered an
extensive view of the surrounding country, disclosed no
sign of any tent. On the following day I myself set off in
a NNE direction, and after travelling five miles struck a
small river on which, by tracing it a short distance, I dis-
covered the camp hidden away in a hollow.

* * *

A: Tell me about your journey back.
R: There is not much to tell. We left the tunnels and
made our way up the mountain. I did not see any more
Kerit. The whole place had an abandoned feel, as if I
had merely imagined it filled with life. (Pause.) I parted
with the Inyanga. He looked troubled, almost hostile to
me, as if I had awoken something that should have been
left sleeping. I made my way south, towards the others'
base camp. It took several days of hard hiking.
A: (Unintelligible).
R: Yes. I occasionally felt I was being followed. But as
immediate events had shown, it had a simple explanation.

* * *

From Wilbusch's Diary
1905
February

28 Last Camp in the Territory
5 a.m. 53° F. 9 p.m. 57° F. Cloudy, rain in the afternoon.
Long march of about 16 miles along the Elgeyo boundary. The rear of the caravan was attacked by a Nandi tribe, and as the porters had no good guns, the loads were stolen and the head man was wounded. Gibbons, I, and some porters pursued the Nandi about 5 miles but could not find them in the wood and returned to the caravan.

* * *

From Gibbons' Report
In the affray, Feraji received a blow on the top of his head with what must have been a spiked instrument, for it left a round hole which by its depth seemed to have penetrated the skull. This blow, which in my opinion would have killed a white man, gave him something in the nature of pain for the first two days, after which he seemed to derive pleasure from it, for it served to illustrate his story from the Ravine as far as Mombassa. Had it not been for his plucky conduct and that of Tanganiko, the boy who came to his rescue, my impression is we would have lost nine loads instead of two.

Unfortunately, we were all out of hearing when the episode occurred.

Accompanied by Mr. Wilbusch, I returned as rapidly as possible as soon as information of the attack was brought me, but to track the thieves in the forest proved as hopeless as I expected it would be, for Swahili porters, through generations of civilization, have lost all the instincts for tracking so marvellously developed in the natural savage. The porters, like the proverbial donkey on his return journey, travelled back so quickly that we were able to catch the train leaving for Nairobi on March 6th, two days earlier than anticipated.

* * *

A: What did you think of Gibbons?
R: (Laughs). You could call him a man of his time. Do you know that Kipling poem? *The White Man's Burden?*
A: I don't recall.
R: Look it up.

* * *

The following—the first stanza of the Kipling poem—was attached to this document.
Take up the White Man's burden –
Send forth the best ye breed –
Go bind your sons to exile
To serve your captives' need;
To wait in heavy harness,
On fluttered folk and wild –

Your new-caught, sullen peoples,
Half-devil and half-child.

* * *

A: Were you a witness to the attack?

R: From afar only. I could not discern the faces of the raiders. Yet I was sure of their intent.

A: Which was?

R: *What will be, was,* the Inyanga had said to me. I think they knew the nature of the expedition, and tried to curtail it. That way, the future would remain only in the realm of possibility, and the past...the past would remain safely dead.

A: So they were successful.

R: I do not know. (Pause). The expedition came to nought. Their report was negative. There was no Jewish settlement in East Africa. And yet...

A: (Unintelligible).

R: Did I awaken something in that lost valley in the Chipchangwane mountains? Did I, by foolishness, allow an opening to form between the two worlds I could see? And did something follow me through it, even now seeking a way back, or a way to...no, I'd rather not indulge in hopeless speculation.

A: It could have been magnificent. A new Jerusalem rising in the mountains of East Africa, a shiny new civilization, dominating all around it, a home of peace and prosperity for all Jews...

R: I saw no peace.

A: (Unintelligible).

R: (Shouting). How did you find me? Who do you work for?

A: Please calm down.

R: Why do you wear those dark glasses?

A: (Unintelligible).

R: I apologise. (Pause). Old memories sometimes ache like old bones.

A: I quite understand.

* * *

From Wilbusch's Diary
1905
March

6 Uganda Railway
Travelled all day, felt rather ill.

7 Mombassa
Arrived in the morning. Waiting for steamer in Hotel Cecil.

8 Mombassa
Steamer arrived today. Went on board later in the afternoon.

9-16 Indian Ocean
Continued my journey to Palestine.

16 Aden
Arrived early in the day. Started at mid-day.

16-21 Red Sea
Continued voyage.

22-26 Port Said
Waiting for steamer to Palestine.

27 Jaffa
Arrived in Palestine.

ACKNOWLEDGMENTS

I am indebted to Marek Kohn's nonfiction work, *Dope Girls*, for the historical background and characters. Anyone who would like to know the true and fascinating stories of Edgar Manning, Brilliant Chang, and Billie Carleton, or indeed the secret history of the London drug underground, should consider it essential reading.

ABOUT THE AUTHOR

Lavie Tidhar is author of *Osama, The Violent Century, A Man Lies Dreaming, Central Station,* and *Unholy Land,* as well as the Bookman Histories trilogy. His latest novels are *By Force Alone,* children's book *The Candy Mafia* and comics mini-series *Adler.* His awards include the World Fantasy Award, the British Fantasy Award, the John W. Campbell Award, the Neukom Prize and the Jerwood Fiction Uncovered Prize.

ALSO BY LAVIE TIDHAR

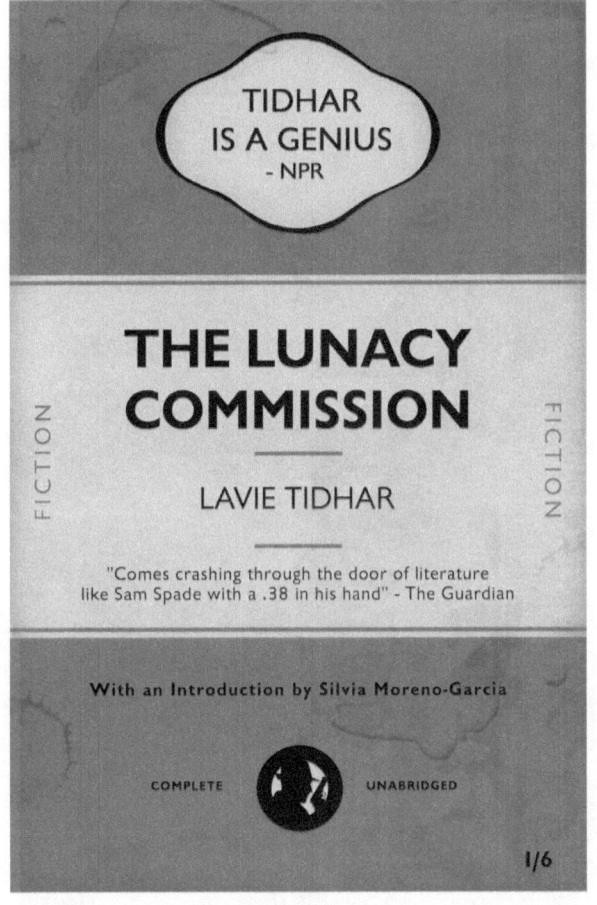

TIDHAR
IS A GENIUS
- NPR

THE LUNACY COMMISSION

FICTION

FICTION

LAVIE TIDHAR

"Comes crashing through the door of literature
like Sam Spade with a .38 in his hand" - The Guardian

With an Introduction by Silvia Moreno-Garcia

COMPLETE   UNABRIDGED

1/6

*Available in paperback and ebook editions
from JABberwocky*

FOR NEWS ABOUT JABBERWOCKY BOOKS AND AUTHORS

Sign up for our newsletter*: http://eepurl.com/b84tDz
visit our website: awfulagent.com/ebooks
or follow us on twitter: @awfulagent

THANKS FOR READING!